About the Author

The author of the novella, just like her heroine, was born and raised in the Soviet Union and emigrated to the United States in the late 1990s. The author is a practicing licensed psychotherapist, for many years she has been working with mentally ill people and with drug and alcohol addiction patients. Therefore, one of her tasks, already as a writer, was to reveal the problem of addiction more deeply and, possibly, influence the prejudice against those who could not cope with life's difficulties, did not find internal and external support, and therefore turned to drugs.

The Girl Who Lost Her Compass

Marie Shantie

The Girl Who Lost Her Compass

Olympia Publishers
London

www.olympiapublishers.com
OLYMPIA PAPERBACK EDITION

A CIP catalogue record for this title is
available from the British Library.

ISBN: 978-1-80074-952-8

First Published in 2023

Olympia Publishers
Tallis House
2 Tallis Street
London
EC4Y 0AB

Printed in Great Britain

Dedication

In loving memory of Sasha Ch.

RUSSIA, '90s

"You've got gonorrhea, bunny!"

"Veronika. My name is Veronika."

The elderly gynecologist had a triple chin and an unkind facial expression. She hostilely stared at the rosebud-cheeked patient, looking her up and down over greasy eyeglasses in a thin frame that accentuated the flabby face.

"How many sexual partners have you had?" she questioned sternly.

Veronika was silent. She didn't know much about gonorrhea; she had read that "this thing" was transmitted only through sex. What if she had something terrible and incurable like AIDS?

"I asked you, how many partners you have had!" The gynecologist raised her voice.

"I don't know."

"Oh, you really don't know how many sex partners you have had?" Angry notes escalated in the doctor's voice. She reminded Veronika of her high school math teacher, who always yelled indignantly and pathetically at everyone who was sitting in the last row.

"So... you don't know? What about your parents? Do they know, or should I tell them?"

"I don't think my parents know exactly how many sex partners I have had," Veronika replied.

"Don't you get clever with me here! I'll ask again. Should I report your gonorrhea to your mother and father?" The gynecologist's voice rose to a shrill siren. Her face turned red with resentment. She believed that her patient was mocking her.

But Veronika didn't even think about joking. It was no laughing matter to her.

Just the thought that her parents would learn about the gonorrhea sent her into panic mode. Instantly, she had difficulty breathing. She imagined her mother screaming at her, and her father sitting with his head in his hands, cringing at his wife's shrieks. Veronika could barely endure her mother's tantrums.

"Don't tell anyone, please," she said quietly. "I beg you, don't! My mother has cancer. I have no father."

That was a lie. Veronika's father was a scientist, a physicist, who practically lived at his institute and was rarely ever home. Her mother, an elementary school teacher, had always been very healthy. Veronika often wondered whether her mother yelled at her first graders like she did at her own daughter, with or without a reason. "Why did you take off your sneakers without cleaning them! Why did you throw them in the middle of the hallway! Why are you so dirty! Did you climb through the street trash, or did you run through the woods! All you do is wander about like a slut!"

"Slut!" the doctor with 40 years' experience suddenly cried out. "No surprise there that you don't have a father, and your mother is sick!"

The gynecologist abruptly rose from the chair, walked to her table by the window, quickly wrote out a prescription, and practically threw it at Veronika.

"Pick it up at a pharmacy and take it as I prescribed it!"

Veronika wanted to ask what gonorrhea was and how is it, in fact, prescribed, but the doctor pointed at the door.

Veronika walked back home through the park, which was especially picturesque in the fall. She loved the town where she was born and grew up, but most of all, she loved this old park with big lakes overgrown with mud, rich in historical and architectural monuments. The main building was the palace where the royal family once lived, now a museum. The park led right to the forest, but Veronika was afraid to go there alone. She turned to the left of the gray river flowing into one of the park lakes and headed toward her house, breathing the delightfully fresh, almost frosty October air and admiring the red-yellow trees, already dusted with snow. Veronika couldn't get the damn gonorrhea out of her head and was in a hurry: 'Go to the pharmacy, get the pills, take them, and never tell anyone about it.'

On the top step at the pharmacy door, she slipped and nearly fell but managed to grab hold of the handle. It opened, and the girl clumsily stumbled inside. Handing the prescription to the old, wrinkled pharmacist with a tired face, she noticed how the woman frowned as she read the doctor's orders. Then, she looked at Veronika.

"Is this for you?"

"Yes, it's for me," Veronika whispered, burning with shame.

"Rotten kids... nothing like in my time." The woman sighed, turned her back, and rummaged through the shelves in search of the medication she needed. As bad luck would

11

have it, a line started growing behind Veronika. In the growing silence, not daring to turn around, she imagined that all these people were looking at her, shaking their heads with disapproval. It felt like hours had passed when finally, the pharmacist returned to the window and proclaimed loudly as if that information was for everybody to hear, "Doxycycline for gonorrhea! Take one hundred milligrams twice a day. Got it?"

"Yes, thank you," Veronika blushed, grabbed the medicine, and put it in her bag. Hunched over and hiding her eyes, she ran to the exit, nearly knocking down a tall man, who was standing at the very end of the line.

"Veronika!" The man pulled off the jacket hood that was covering half of his face and grabbed her by the shoulders.

She looked up and saw his kind, radiant smile. How she had been yearning for that smile and for those gray, lustrous eyes! Sasha... A bitter lump rolled up in her throat. Veronika buried her face in his chest and burst into tears.

"Well, well, well, little one... What's wrong?" He hugged her and stroked her hair. "Did something happen?"

Veronika shook her head. If only she could tell him! So much had happened to her since they broke up a year and a half ago. She pulled away and peered at Sasha from under her eyebrows.

"I better go."

"Where are you going? Wait! I just need to get my granny's medicine!" Sasha pulled out the prescription from his pocket. "M O R P H I N E," he spelled the doctor's writing out loud. "Look at me, I'm no M.D., but I can read scribble!" He grinned and continued, "Mor-phine! Like a dope fiend! In the poppy field! All my pain is healed! This is everything I dreamed!" He laughed, delighted at his own little rhyme. "Allow me to introduce myself! Famous poet and sort of a scribbler, too, just a different kind," Sasha made a motion with his hand as if raising a hat, then he bowed. "MC Sasha, the Scribbler! At your service!"

Veronika laughed and wiped her tears.

"I'll wait for you outside," she said, looking at the line.

"Yes, yes! I'll be quick."

Veronika went out onto the porch. Cold air immediately whipped her face, still wet with tears. She shrunk her head into her collar and smiled. She loved Sasha's jokes, loved when he made her laugh and fooled around... when they were still in school. Back then, Sasha used to approach her during recess. In the classroom, in front of everybody, he would lean over and, gently holding her, slowly and sensually kiss her on the lips. Veronika would melt, feeling butterflies in her stomach, the ones she'd heard so much about. He looked into her eyes, asked how she was doing, and how her day was going. He used to gently pick her up and, still kissing her, take her out of the classroom. He didn't give a damn that his behavior appalled his teachers. He was in love with Veronika, and she was in love with him like a cat in spring. Besides, she was flattered that Sasha, the most popular boy in school, chose her.

It all started the end of August of that memorable summer. They went kayaking and spent nights in tents in the woods, and they fished and cooked fish to eat. One quiet evening by the fire, Veronika was reading Sasha's fortune with playing cards. With a serious face, she announced some nonsense. Sasha was admiring her. He watched how she continually brushed away her naughty bangs with her thin, graceful hands. He inhaled the scent of her skin, which smelled of sweet strawberries. Unable to restrain himself, he kissed her and said that he would be staying the night. Veronika playfully dodged and teased him.

"Are you afraid to sleep alone in your tent?"

"Yeah, I'm afraid! I'm afraid of the big bad wolf. Will you take me in?"

Veronika laughed louder, making Sasha even more excited. His lips passionately touched her lips, and then he was no longer able to stop.

"And now," he whispered hoarsely, "the most important part."

And he slipped his hand under her clothes.

After that night, Sasha followed his new girlfriend around like a lovesick puppy. Their love grew stronger at the forest edges, in thorny bushes, and in the cold river. Veronika was incredibly loving, passionate, and available. Her alluring smile and scent drove Sasha's raging teenage hormones insane. He wanted to have her, and at the same time, he wanted to give her everything he could, if only to prolong this euphoria together.

The day before returning home, they vowed eternal love and sealed their union with blood. Sasha took out a razor blade, rolled up his sleeve, and with a sharp movement made a vertical cut on his wrist.

"Hey, what are you doing?" exclaimed Veronika. The sight of blood nauseated her.

"It's necessary. Now, your turn!" he commanded.

"I'm afraid you'll cut a vein. Can it be just a finger?" She handed him the ring finger of her right hand and closed her eyes. The sharp pain from the cut made her cry out. But the very next moment, she pressed her bleeding finger to his hand.

That same evening, when they were lying in bed in his room in his grandparents' apartment, with whom he lived, Sasha told Veronika about his secret hiding place.

"It's here, in the speaker," Sasha said quietly, nodding toward the stereo. "No one knows about it except me and you."

"Hm, and what are you keeping there?"

"Five hundred bucks and some other small things."

When Veronika was about to leave, Sasha handed her the key to the apartment.

"My grandparents have gone on a business trip for two weeks. Tomorrow, I'm going to Saint Petersburg to see my father. Come over the day after!"

"See how he trusts me!" boasted Veronika to her best friend Alina that evening after telling her that Sasha had shared an important secret with her and given her the key.

Alina didn't express any enthusiasm. Instead, she asked, looking firmly at Veronika, "Why do you even need this immature boy?" Sasha, who was younger than both of them, belonged to the rich crowd. He always had money, and he wore famous designers' clothes. Sasha's grandparents, his mother's parents, were scientists at the local institute of nuclear physics. When Sasha was nine years old, his mother divorced his father and married another man. The new husband demanded that she, a cardiologist by profession, leave the hospital and become a housewife. Reluctantly, she did. They had a son, and Sasha's mother devoted all her time to his little brother.

Sasha's stepfather didn't like him from the start and insisted that he live with his grandparents from now on. Every Sunday, when his mother dropped by for a half-hour to see him, Sasha experienced pain and resentment, which made him cry. He knew that his mother was visiting him furtively, without telling her new husband.

After the divorce, Sasha's father married a much younger woman. She was quite superficial, a gold-digger. She called herself a "socialite" and "the first party girl of Saint Petersburg." She attended all the popular gatherings and parties in the city. Of course, the stepmother didn't care about Sasha, just like she didn't care about his father, whom she had married for his money. Sasha's father had his own business and connections in the criminal world. Without any questions, he would give his son money, and Sasha would spend it on Veronika. He took his girlfriend to restaurants and ordered expensive food and wine. He was always surrounded by friends, who were not opposed to eating and drinking for free and, while they were at it, meeting girls, who were also always around Sasha or rather, around his wallet.

"He doesn't give you any money, and he doesn't buy you presents," Alina continued to work her friend.

She was right, but Veronika became defensive.

"He takes me to restaurants!"

"So what? You have one dress, one skirt, and two blouses, and those are your mother's; your parents have no money for new clothes. Let him buy you a fur coat! Maybe you should ask him?"

"No, I just can't," said Veronika. She was too proud to ask.

"Listen," Alina continued to insist, "if he doesn't offer, then you have to take action!"

"Damn it, I can't ask him for money, Alina!"

"That's not what I'm asking you to do!"

"What then?"

"Didn't he tell you where the money is?"

Veronika stared blankly at her friend.

"You think…"

"Yes, I know it!"

Veronika could not believe what she was hearing, but Alina talked and talked, trying to convince her. She said that Sasha didn't want to straight-up offer her money and, therefore, told her about his hiding spot, gave her the key, and informed her that there would be no one at home. All this was an obvious hint. Having promised her friend that she would come break into the apartment with her, Alina added that they needed to do it tomorrow since there would be no other opportunity like that. "Wouldn't you like money? Personally, I don't want to walk in old boots and light coat for fall when it's so freaking cold outside." Alina made a compelling argument.

The anticipation of an adventure finally overcame apprehensions and doubts, and Veronika agreed.

The next day, the girls met at Sasha's building entrance. They punched the familiar combination on the buzzer and went inside. Trying not to make noise just in case, the girls climbed the stairs to the fifth floor. Veronika reluctantly pulled out the apartment key from her pocket. Feeling her friend's uncertainty, Alina hissed, "Give it to me!"

She grabbed the key from Veronika's trembling hands, deftly inserted it into the lock, and tried to turn it, but it didn't work.

"You have to put pressure on it," Veronika whispered, remembering how Sasha always leaned on the door to open it.

"What?" Alina didn't hear her.

"Nothing! Just push it with your shoulder!"

That's when they heard the front door of the neighbor's apartment unlock. The girls looked at each other nervously, realizing that they wouldn't have the time to do anything. The neighbor's door opened, and a gray head stuck out. An old man squinted blindly.

"Damn it!" Veronika proclaimed loudly, taking the key from her friend. "It's jammed again! I've had enough of this! I gotta tell my grandfather to fix this stupid door already! Oh, hello!" she turned to the neighbor, as if she had just noticed him. The old man, not suspecting anything, nodded, stepped out of his apartment, locked it, and meandered down the stairs.

"I didn't know you were that resourceful, my dear!"

Veronika was pleased to receive a compliment from Alina. She herself was surprised how quickly she managed to make up something on the spot, but there was no time to think about it. Veronika pressed on the door, and, hallelujah, it opened. The girls entered the hallway and turned on the lights. Veronika was about to go inside, but Alina whispered dramatically, "Stop! Take off your sneakers, or you'll leave footprints!"

The girls took off their shoes and ran together into Sasha's room. As they took the money out of the speaker, excitement overwhelmed them.

"Veronika, do you maybe know where they keep their

mop? Go clean the hallway. You still managed to track it all up with your shoes!"

"Then maybe we'll also have some tea after we finish cleaning?" laughed Veronika.

"Why the hell not?" Alina responded and promptly went into the kitchen, like an unconcerned thief. She put some water in the kettle, put it on the stove, and turned on the gas.

"Are there any sweets here?"

After the tea and thorough cleaning in the kitchen, the girls locked the apartment and left the building. It was chilly outside, but adrenaline continued to rush through their veins so strongly that they didn't feel the cold. Choking with laughter, the girls ran toward the forest as fast as they could, non-stop for several minutes. The farther they got from the building, the louder they laughed and shouted. Having exhausted themselves, they stopped to catch their breaths, hugged, and kissed.

"That was something!"

"Girl! So awesome!"

"Unreal! We are the coolest criminals ever! We are fearless!"

"Criminal masterminds! We did it!"

"It was even cooler than the kiosk!"

"Hell, yeah! So much cooler!"

***

The incident with the food kiosk happened a few months ago. Late one evening, Alina and Veronika were walking along the road to the park where they loved to stroll and share their innermost feelings, mainly about guys. At the crossroads, under the dully glowing streetlight, they stopped to share a cigarette. Alina took the first pull and handed it to her friend. Veronika remembered how one of her classmates taught her to smoke: inhale the smoke, hold it in, and… Before she could even inhale, Alina snatched the cigarette from her mouth.

"Give me that! You don't know how it's done, anyway!"

Suddenly, they noticed two black figures in the dark, standing by the lonely food kiosk, which had closed for the night. Almost immediately they heard a voice.

"Veronika! Is that you?"

The silhouettes quickly approached. Under the street light, Veronika and Alina recognized the boys from school—Ivan and Pavel. Pavel had a funny nickname: Pavel-the-Orphan.

"Oh!" the girls rejoiced, "It's you. You scared us, you know!"

"Why are you wandering through empty streets at such a late hour?" Ivan frowned.

"No reason; we're just walking, chatting," Veronika replied calmly. "What are you doing here?"

"We're going to rob that food stand!"

"What do you mean?" the girls asked simultaneously and stared at them.

"Well, we're gonna relieve it of some food, take what we can! Wanna come with us? See, there's an iron bolt on it? And here, on the right, you see? The alarm is on. We'll throw a rock at it and hide. And you run to that building across from it; go behind the corner. You'll be on the lookout."

The girls remained shocked for a minute, and then they understood each other. Both wanted Snickers and Bounty chocolate bars, chewing gum, and Coca-Cola, which they could only dream about when they watched American TV shows. They both knew that all this could be found at that kiosk. Without much further thought, they rushed to the corner of the building that Ivan and Pavel-the-Orphan had pointed out. The girls froze and held their breaths, looking at the boys hovering around the kiosk.

Finally, Ivan took out a stone from his pocket and threw it at the red light at the roof of the stand. The alarm went off, blasting like a rock concert.

Oooo-oo-oo-oo!

The boys quickly made their way to the corner, where the girls were nervously shifting their feet, and all four froze, pressed up against the wall. The police did not make them wait too long: the patrol made its appearance in just a minute's time. The guys stood motionless, watching from around the corner how the policemen jumped out of the old cop car and ran to the kiosk. Veronika could hear her heart pounding like crazy. Fearing that she would laugh if she looked at her accomplices, she stared at the ground. The alarm stopped howling, and now the robbers could clearly hear the policemen cursing in the silence of the dark quiet street. They checked around the hut some more and then climbed back into the car, per their superior's order, who had been standing by the car the entire time. The car drove away in the direction of the police station, which was only two blocks away. The girls gasped in amazed delight.

"Oh, shit! That was crazy! Now what?"

Without answering, the boys rushed back to the kiosk. This time, Pavel-the-Orphan pulled a stone from his pocket and tossed it at the red light above the stand. It instantly went off again. Under its deafening wails, the boys galloped back to the girls along the already familiar path.

This time, they waited four minutes for the patrol. The cop car drove over slowly, the cops lazily tumbled out, and looked around. They didn't even approach the food stand. Not noticing anything criminal, they cussed and left again.

The girls were excited and could barely hold back a nervous laugh. They were having so much fun although they were a little scared. Meanwhile, Ivan and Pavel-the-Orphan, looking around, trotted up to the food stand one more time. Ivan took out another stone.

Oooo-oo-oo-oo! went the alarm. Around the corner, all four stood, waiting for the patrol, but the police were in no hurry this time. The alarm went off for about seven minutes, lights came on in several windows of the nearest building, and the screaming siren finally stopped. The police didn't show.

"Follow me!" commanded Ivan.

He ran to the food stand in a hurry.

"Come on, you two," Pavel whispered to the girls. "Come with us."

He followed his friend.

Veronika hesitated for a second, but Alina pulled her sleeve.

"Let's go, or we don't get anything! We didn't act like lookouts for nothing!"

They ran to the food stand. The boys knowingly removed the deadbolt, opened the door, and all four stared stupidly at the boxes with foreign letters—the embodiment of the "American dream" for Soviet teenagers. Seconds later, chocolate bars, gum, chips and soda—oh, yeah, sweet Coca-Cola—all of it went into the plastic bags that Pavel-the-Orphan was clever enough to bring with him.

"Now, we scatter in different directions! Keep away from the houses so that the neighbors don't bust us," Ivan said quietly and clearly.

The boys vanished so quickly toward the park that Veronika and Alina were a little confused at first. However, the heavy bags of loot reminded them of the danger, and the girls took off running in the opposite direction from the boys. Only a few blocks away, they stopped, out of breath, sat down on a bench, laughed, and looked inside the bags filled with their treasures...

***

The girls split the money they had stolen from Sasha in half. That seemed fair. Veronika bought herself a short leopard fur coat, a pair of fashionable high platform boots, and a checkered dress. She also got herself a simple wristwatch with a black-and-white Mickey Mouse on the dial. Alina made fun of it, chuckling something like, "It's childish!" Still, Veronika wore it all the time, almost without taking it off. She was not at all proud of how she got to own her first watch, but it reminded her of Sasha.

Veronika could no longer be with Sasha. She realized this as soon as she brought the new things home. It's not that she was afraid of her boyfriend's reaction when he realized who took the money from the secret spot. Rather, she was terribly ashamed of what she had done: she knew that she wouldn't be able to look him in the eye. She spun Sasha some story on the phone, saying that she had fallen in love with someone else and no longer wanted to see him.

At first, Veronika really missed her ex-boyfriend and sometimes she dialed his home phone. She hoped Sasha still did not have caller ID and wouldn't know it was her when he picked up. She just remained quiet on the phone and listened to his voice saying "hello" until he hung up.

Veronika had never completed high school but instead earned a GED, which allowed her to enroll in a community college to study economics. She wasn't stupid or lazy. She just didn't like high school, so finishing it did not seem like an option.

A new life began in college and with new friends—her classmates. She thought about Sasha less and less. The guys in college invited her to the movies, exhibitions, and parties after school. Veronika had several admirers at once, who helped her cheat on homework and assisted her in preparing for exams. Among her female classmates, on the contrary, she couldn't make any friends. They all seemed either arrogant or envious. They stared and greeted her condescendingly.

The college professors differed from her high school teachers. They didn't yell, but Veronika felt indifference and wasn't even sure if they noticed her.

Studying was hard for Veronika. Economics and related subjects didn't interest her at all. Honestly, she had no idea what she was interested in and was genuinely surprised by friends and relatives who attended universities and studied day and night to become doctors, teachers, and scientists. In her free time, Veronika still met with her best friend Alina. As they both liked to say, they were "cruising for a bruising."

The girls differed considerably in appearance and in personality. The first eye-catching thing about Veronika was her stunning ginger hair, which she got from her father and which her mother used to braid, explaining to Veronika that kids would tease her for her red hair if it were too noticeable. She also had her father's gray eyes, which turned completely black when she became excited, angry, or fearful. Veronika didn't like to notice the resemblance to her mother, if any. She wasn't particularly tall or slender, but there was some elusive attractiveness, something sensual, something inexplicably seductive in her shining eyes, gestures, and gait. More often than not, Veronika was talkative and cheerful, and she always had a smile on her face, even in her sleep.

Alina was a brown-eyed blonde with classical features. Glamorous and beautiful like the models on magazine covers, she was also self-assured and level-headed. Boys her age didn't even dare to approach such a beauty. Alina, unlike Veronika, got straight As in school and had a clear goal: find a rich "sugar daddy" with his own business, a big apartment in the center of Saint Petersburg or Moscow, and a good, new foreign car.

Veronika seemed to have no goals. But she had a dream she didn't tell anyone about.

***

One warm Saturday evening, the girls were walking along

the brightly lit Moscow Avenue in Saint Petersburg.

"Would you like to buy some flowers, pretty ladies?"

Two handsome Uzbek men selling fresh roses and tulips smiled at them from the kiosk. The girls slowed down a little.

"Girls don't buy flowers," Alina answered boldly in her usual manner to the one who spoke. "They accept them!"

"In this case," the merchant smiled mysteriously, "I give you these beautiful roses." And he handed Alina a whole armful.

She took the bouquet with a regal look and smiled at the men seductively.

"Beautiful girls, we invite you to a restaurant!"

The girls looked at each other.

"Why not?" Veronika read the familiar expression on Alina's face and thought to herself, 'At least we'll eat for free.' And she nodded, agreeing approvingly.

The Uzbeks, who introduced themselves as Amid and Azamat, turned out to be friendly and polite, shared that they sold cosmetics in the market during the day and flowers on the street in the evenings. They generously treated the girls to steak kebabs, fries, ice cream, and coffee. When the men invited Alina and Veronika to their home to "have a glass of wine," the girls agreed. In their one-room apartment, the young men showed Veronika and Alina some of the goods that they kept in a closet in the hallway, explaining that the merchandise was "for a sale." Veronika and Alina eagerly looked at the shiny packs with lipstick, eye shadows, mascara, and jars of cream for hands and face.

"Veronika," Alina suddenly said, setting the glass of wine aside, "let's go to the kitchen and chat for a minute."

In the kitchen, she whispered to Veronika's ear: "Do you understand why I brought you here?"

"Not really. If you like one of them, he is yours. I don't like them that much…"

"No, you idiot! I'm not interested in these two, either. But we didn't come here for nothing. Did you see how many cosmetics they have? Do you think they would share some with us?"

"I doubt that. They are peddlers."

"Exactly. Therefore, we gotta help them part with a couple of boxes. They won't even notice. And you know how much we can get for one such box? At the least, you'll be able to buy a dress for the New Year's celebration and shoes for the spring. Okay? Listen to me. You need to distract both of them somehow while I pretend that I feel sick and need to use the bathroom. Instead of going there, I'll grab a box or two in the hallway and leave it somewhere safe in the building. Understand the plan?"

"Not really. How can I distract them?"

"Well, think of something! Use your imagination!" Alina laughed, covering her mouth with her hand.

"Got cards, boys?" Veronika asked the men cheerfully, returning to the room. "I'm gonna read you your fortunes."

"Oh, is that so? Do you really know how to read cards? And what is the reading gonna be about?"

"Love, of course!"

Almost immediately, a deck of cards appeared from somewhere, and Veronika began to shuffle it, not very skillfully, but with a confident look.

"I think Alina's not feeling so good; she needs to use the bathroom," she mentioned casually.

She was enthusiastically predicting Azamat's fate, by inventing everything right on the go, when Alina returned and winked slightly at her friend.

"Everything good?" asked Veronika cautiously.

"Everything's great. No problem," Alina answered, sitting down in a chair like a queen. A triumphant smile lit up her face.

Veronika breathed a sigh of relief and chirped breezily.

"Let's dance, boys!" And then she jumped up, ran up to the tape recorder, and put on a cassette of her favorite band, Technology.

They slowly and smoothly moved in pairs to *Strange Dances*. Veronika was hanging on Azamat; Alina was embracing Amid. The men, however, behaved politely and didn't make passes. They dealt with the police from time to time and knew, as foreigners in this city they needed to be careful with Russian women. When Veronika and Alina said that it was time for them to go home, the men called a taxi and gave the girls money for it. They kissed both girls goodbye on the cheek and thanked them for the wonderful evening.

The boxes that Alina had pulled out from the hospitable apartment were waiting for the girls, hidden in a dark corner behind the garbage chute. Rejoicing at what "cool criminals" they were and chuckling at the "poor suckers," they had so easily conned, the girls got into the taxi.

***

Her mother had no idea how Veronika got to college every day, or didn't want to know because she couldn't give her money, anyway, even for the bus. She didn't ask her daughter anything, and Veronika told her nothing. It's not like she could tell her mother that she hitched rides instead of taking the bus. At eight on the dot, she was already standing at the bus stop trying to hitchhike to college by nine. First, she stuck out her thumb only at expensive-looking imported cars, hoping that their owners were unlikely to need money and, therefore, would take her to her destination for free. If no foreign cars came along or they didn't stop, she would try to thumb a ride from anybody who passed by.

"Are you going to Saint Petersburg? Can you drop me off just for a 'thank you'?" she would ask in a sweet voice.

She returned home from school the same way. Most often, she was lucky. The drivers were decent people and just wanted to converse with someone along the way. Veronika could chat away, talking anyone's ear off, so that in the end, everyone was happy. They gave her rides for free and only infrequently asked for her number. For such cases, she had invented a non-existent number, which she would quickly recite. But sometimes, it didn't go smoothly: at the final destination, a few drivers would unzip their pants and demand that she "return the favor" or something similar. Those times, Veronika jumped out of the car as fast as she could.

Once, she was waiting at a bus stop in Saint Petersburg for more than an hour, trying to catch a ride. It was a cold late autumn day. She had no money at all and had no choice but to try to catch any passing car. She was so tired and cold that when a beautiful black Mercedes suddenly stopped in front of her, Veronika was ready to jump inside without hesitation. The tinted window on the front door rolled down, and she could see that there were three people inside. Veronika remembered her rule: not to get into a car if there was someone else in it besides the driver.

At that moment, the plump brown-haired driver asked.

"Where are you going, miss?"

She could barely feel her feet in her cheap light boots that were not in any way intended for such weather and automatically blurted out the address. She just wanted to get home as soon as possible.

"We're going that way, too. Hop in!"

Veronika ignored her rule and got into the back seat next to a blue-eyed, brown-haired young man around 20 years old. He smiled broadly, revealing yellowed teeth, probably from smoking too much.

Music was playing loudly in the car, the passengers, however, were quiet: they didn't ask her any questions, they didn't ask for her phone number, they just shared their names and asked her hers. Veronika gradually warmed up and relaxed. At a familiar fork on the way home, though, the Mercedes suddenly turned not into her town, but into the next one.

"You're going the wrong way!" the girl said, her senses suddenly alert and a nervousness creeping into her stomach.

"It's fine, baby girl, we just need some gas, that's all. Got it?"

The car drove up to a small motel with a gas station. The blue-eyed man, whose name was Mikhail, if Veronika remembered correctly, suggested waiting in the cafe while the others pumped the gas. Veronika followed him.

However, there was no cafe. Just a hotel room. Gently

pushing her inside, Mikhail entered the room too and stood by the door, letting the driver, the second passenger and four other strange men in.

Then, he locked the door; one of the men hurried to the window, closed the curtains, and put a full glass of vodka in front of Veronika.

"I don't drink," she said loudly and clearly, even though the fear inside her was all she could feel.

She saw the grins on their faces.

"You have to pay for the ride, girl," said the one who closed the curtains. He smiled disgustingly and added, "Why else would you get into the car?"

Veronika realized that she was trapped: she had nowhere to run and no way to ask for help. Tears filled her eyes, yet she gathered up her courage and, restraining her trembling voice, spoke up.

"Guys, my boyfriend in Saint Petersburg is a known gangsta! He knows everyone! So, you better not play with fire. Better let me go!"

The men all laughed. Veronika desperately looked at the glass of vodka in front of her. 'What now? What can I do? I'm running out of time!' Her mind was racing.

Blue Eyes slowly began to unfasten his belt.

"Guys, don't, I beg you. I implore you, please!" Veronika cried out with anguish, recalling the advice from some women's magazines on how to talk with potential rapists. "After all, you all have mothers or sisters! What if someone did this to them?"

Veronika's ranting didn't appeal to them. One moved closer, onto the bed, directly opposite the table, at which she was sitting. The other went to the door, pulled the handle,

31

making sure that it was locked. The third, holding a glass of vodka in his hands, was already hanging over her, panting and reeking of booze.

Veronika squeezed into the chair and cried. She begged them again and again not to touch her, to let her go. She said that she didn't want this, that it was wrong. But her pleas seemed to excite them even more. Aroused, ready to attack, they smiled smugly, clucked their tongues, made dirty jokes, and, following Mikhail's example, also began to open their flies.

Instinctively, she determined that he was the leader here.

"I want to talk to you!" Veronika suddenly turned to him and quietly added, "Please... Can we go somewhere where we'll be alone?"

She had no idea what she would say next. She simply felt that she needed to speak to him and no one else.

"I need to tell you something," she repeated, noticing that she had gotten his attention. Mikhail looked at her intently and then turned to his friends.

"Leave me with the girl for a short while."

They implicitly obeyed.

When they left, Veronika spoke smoothly.

"Listen, I'm not stupid. Nor am I a prostitute or a slut. Do you know why I got into the car with you?" She looked with dreamy eyes right at Mikhail, as if about to reveal a great secret.

"Why?" he looked surprised.

"Because," Veronika hesitated, "because I liked your eyes!"

She blurted out the first thing that came to her mind, but

a second later, she took control of herself, and the words just started pouring themselves.

"You have very beautiful and expressive eyes. As soon as I saw them, I wanted to meet you. I would have never gotten into a car with three guys or even two. Never! However, just one look at you, and I realized that you were the one I'd always wanted, the one I saw in my dreams and fantasies, the one I desired... like I do now... but you brought your friends here. Why? I want only you!" Veronika even felt brave enough to gently touch his hand.

"Hm... really?" Blue Eyes looked at her suspiciously.

"Yes! This is very serious for me! Can we just be together, only me and you? You don't want someone else to touch me, do you? I beg you, don't let them!"

"Um... even after everything that went on here? Do you want to be with me, anyway?"

"Yes. Only with you. Even more so. If after everything that's happened, you can make it so that I'm only with you, then... then... you'll be a real hero in my eyes!"

Without saying another word, Mikhail left the room, almost immediately returned and said, "Okay, let's go! We'll take you home, and then I will meet you alone."

Still not believing her luck, Veronika followed Mikhail. Slipping past the others, who stood in the hallway with sour faces, and trying not to look at them, she jumped into the back seat. With a victorious look on his face, the 'winner' sat next to her and casually put his hand on her shoulders. The same driver slammed the front door behind the second passenger, squeezed behind the wheel, and drove them along the snow-banked highway. A vile smell of tobacco and fumes and loud Russian *chanson* that Veronika could not stand filled the car, but she was just overjoyed. She blissfully breathed in the frosty air, drifting inside as her car companions opened the windows to throw out their cigarette butts. She had gotten out of a real nasty bind. She had succeeded in overcoming the threat, she had come out on top!

"Give me your number," Mikhail reminded her when they stopped not far from Veronika's house. He looked at her lustily, almost with love. "I'll call you tomorrow."

She told him the usual fake number, kissed him on the cheek as if he really were her boyfriend, and darted out of the car.

***

Of course, she didn't say anything to her mother, but on the way to the new nightclub in town, she shared all the near-rape details with her closest friend. Alina listened, now and then throwing wide-eyed glances at Veronika, and at the end of the story, exclaimed with admiration, "Wow, girl, what a thing!" But then, she couldn't resist and quipped: "Where did such talent, such mastery, such deep knowledge in psychology come from?"

Alina was being ironic because she was a little envious. She wasn't always that lucky when it came to free rides from their town to Saint Petersburg and back…

They stopped, Alina took out a pack of Parliaments and said to Veronika, "Okay, let's have a smoke."

Veronika enjoyed their little ritual—sharing a cigarette—but, knowing that she would have to take off her mittens in the cold, she shivered. Alina pointed toward the nearest five-story building. They went inside. The lobby was dark and dirty and stank of garbage and cat urine. The two of them pressed themselves against a barely functioning radiator. They needed to warm up a little at least: for the club, they both wore thin, off-season leggings and short close-fitting skirts. Alina skillfully lit a cigarette, took a drag, and handed it to Veronika. She gathered smoke into her lungs and held her breath: she liked it when her head began to spin for a few seconds, and the ground seemed to crumble under her feet. It was quiet in the building, and for a moment, Veronika felt a light buzz. The cigarette went out, Alina repeatedly struck the lighter, and the flame lit up the ragged, stained wall. On it was written in large, loose bright red letters, apparently in lipstick, the word BITCH.

In order not to lose the warmth they had obtained with such difficulty, they ran out of the building and almost galloped to the club. Deep down, each girl hoped to find a guy there, not just any guy, but a knight in shining armor! If not that, then one in a sparkling Mercedes or the latest model BMW. Veronika imagined how she would stand at the bar, drink Martini and Rossi, and suddenly catch a glance of a bearded brown-haired man who looked a bit like her father. From the way that stranger examined her with his impudent gaze, undressed her with his eyes, she felt increasing arousal, heat spreading throughout her body. The "knight" would swagger up to her, confidently take her hand, and lead her to the center of the dance floor. They would move a little to the music, and then he would passionately kiss her on the lips, pick her up in his arms, and take her outside to his white Mercedes. Already on the go, he would casually instruct the driver: "To the justice of the peace!"

In her fantasy, Alina, too, drank "Martini and Rossi" at the bar and imagined herself with a brown-haired man in a sparkling Mercedes. The rest of the dream differed from Veronika's, starting with the bar, which most certainly would be in a fashionable, chic nightclub. There, she would stand, sipping a cocktail, dressed in Gucci, and wearing shimmering diamond earrings. The man of her dreams, as Alina imagined, was always blue-eyed with silver strands in his hair. Their eyes would meet. He would slowly approach her, kiss her gracefully extended hand, and just like that, slide a golden ring with a five-carat diamond—no less!—on her finger. He then would take her to his luxurious mansion, where a Jacuzzi with red rose petals awaited.

Fifteen to sixteen-year-old pimpled teenagers crowded around the club, in reality, smoking cigarettes and drinking beer from the cans. Muffled techno beats were coming out of the building. They were blocking the way, and the girls barely squeezed through the crowd near the door. A square-shouldered, tall bouncer guarded the entrance.

"Ladies are free!" he yelled, letting Alina and Veronika in. They hung up their coats on the rack near the door, and, looking curiously around, walked inside a room with thundering dance music and flashing disco lights. Long-legged, anorexic-looking girls, mostly blondes and a couple with raven-colored hair, all provocatively wearing high heels and displaying languid faces, minced around on the dance floor. Older men in expensive suits, ties, and Rolexes slumped in chairs, looking like VIPs. Half-naked dancers wriggled like cobras in cages under the ceiling, casting calculated predatory glances at the visitors. Feeling timid, Alina and Veronika walked over to the empty bar and sat on the high chairs. While hoping that one of the men in suits would pay them some attention and treat them to a cocktail, the girlfriends pretended to watch the dancers and stared at the dance floor. They didn't have to wait that long.

"Hello, girls! I'm Konstantin." A fair-haired man, who appeared somewhere from the depths of the hall, introduced himself. He looked like the lead singer of the Mumiy Troll band. "What will you be drinking tonight?"

"Martini and Rossi," Alina and Veronika answered simultaneously.

"Two martinis for the ladies!" Konstantin waved his hand to the bartender.

Having sipped a little from her glass, Veronika first felt bitterness in her mouth and then pleasant warmth flooding her veins. Meanwhile, Konstantin had moved closer to Alina, who was trying to shout over the roaring techno, and in an unnaturally high-pitched voice, was telling him something about her school. Veronika felt a bit resentful. Once again, she looked around the dance floor, at the dull interior, at the men at the tables, and realized that she was disappointed: the men were all kind of lardy, flabby, much older, and much less attractive than their new friend, Konstantin.

"What is love? Baby, don't hurt me!" Veronika perked up when the first words floated across the room. It was her favorite musician, Haddaway's "Don't hurt me no more!" She really wanted to dance to this cool electric tune, but Konstantin had already taken Alina to the dance floor. Skinny girls, mostly dancing alone, sometimes with overweight sugar daddies, started swaying their hips with affectation. Not without jealousy, Veronika watched Alina passionately press up against Konstantin. She was bored and wanted to go home, curl up in her warm bed, and go to sleep. But first, she wanted to eat. Her mother was a great cook, but she didn't cook often; they bought meat only for holidays and mostly ate toast and cheese sandwiches. Veronika had loved cheese since she was little. She remembered how when she was six, her mother would always say, giving her a slice, "Eat while we have it, daughter. Maybe it's the last time."

Until now, Veronika ate cheese at every opportunity, gently laying it on thick slices of bread and butter.

"Another cocktail?" The bartender's voice brought her back to reality.

Veronika shook her head and asked.

"Do you have potato chips?" She had already begun having hunger pangs.

The bartender handed her a menu. There were chips, the nuts that she liked so much, and French fries that she had tried only once. Her stomach growled harder. Veronika desperately glanced at Alina, still dancing with Konstantin. She had no money so she had to count on her friend. When the song ended, Alina majestically approached the bar.

"Can you ask him to buy us some chips and crab sticks?" Veronika yelled into her friend's ear.

"Okay, no problem!" said Alina and in a possessive manner passed the request to Konstantin.

Veronika felt an urge to compete with her girlfriend. When Konstantin offered to take them both home, she was the first to jump into the passenger seat of his brand-new

Ford. She could feel how annoyed Alina was because she had to sit in the back.

"So, who needs to get where?" asked Konstantin.

Before Veronika opened her mouth, Alina quickly gave him Veronika's address.

"I live on Karl Marx Avenue, but if it's more convenient for you to give Alina a ride first, she lives on 4 Red Army Street," Veronika clarified briefly because she had figured out her girlfriend's scheme.

Veronika, just like Alina, hoped that Konstantin would first drop off the other girl so she would be left alone with him. And, of course, she felt her heart skip a beat when he started driving to Alina's address. She was afraid to turn to Alina because she understood perfectly that her friend was mad at both of them, especially, of course, at her. Head up, Alina proudly got out of the automobile and slammed the car door. Veronika made a face at her back and then gently looked at the driver and repeated her address. Konstantin nodded, without saying a word.

Veronika was already going through various romantic scenarios in her head and barely managed to notice that the car had turned in the opposite direction from her house, toward the forest.

"Hey," trying to hide her concern, she said, "you're going the wrong way!"

But Konstantin didn't react at all; on the contrary, he even sped up.

"My house is not that way!" Veronika was already quite scared, remembering what had happened with Mikhail. The driver was silent, and the car was still rushing toward the woodland.

"Where are you taking me?" cried Veronika. She felt helpless and terrified—again!

Not looking at her, Konstantin turned on the music, and the speakers blew up with Mumiy Troll's "Flow away." From this weird coincidence, from the sounds of strange, hopped-up music, from the fact that he didn't even hear her, she suddenly felt how absurd and surreal this situation was! It suddenly dawned on her that she was in a car that was racing God knows where with God knows who.

Konstantin drove into the forest, stopped on the side of the road and turned off the engine. Veronika, petrified, didn't have a second to think when he unexpectedly turned to her, put a knife that came from nowhere to her throat, and quietly said, "Wanna play?"

His face was covered with white-red spots and drops of sweat. He had a vacant expression in his eyes like there was nothing there. It's as if he had turned into a different person and no longer even looked like the lead of the popular band.

Veronika sat in a stupor, dismayed. The blade of the knife rested sharply against her neck, and she was afraid to move. A single thought pounded in her head, 'Oh, God, he's a maniac!'

With his free hand, he began to unfasten his pants. A memory and a sense of déjà vu clicked in Veronika's mind, and she cried out in a tense voice, "No, no, wait!"

"And what shall we wait for?" said Konstantin in the same quiet and sinister voice.

"I gotta talk to you."

Scraps of phrases lingered in Veronika's head, more advice from those magazines for women: what to do if you were attacked by a sex-crazed psycho. Tell him to imagine that someone could do the same with his sister or mother as he was now with her. Damn, no, that didn't work the other time! Yes! She could say that she had AIDS. He might just wear a condom. Or… what was it? She could pretend that she was crazy! Or ask him if he can see her… because she is invisible. No, no! That's no good! All this was stupid nonsense.

"So, what do you want to talk to me about?" he asked in a toneless voice.

Veronika flinched, and suddenly, it just slipped out.

"Kant!"

Konstantin blinked slowly. Lessening the pressure of the knife, he stared at the girl.

"About wha-aat?" he asked, as if recovering. "About Kant?"

"Yes! About Kant!" Veronika confirmed as if nothing with the knife, with his zipper, or with his behavior had happened and, not letting him come to his senses, asked the first question that came to mind.

"Do you like his theories?"

The effect of surprise worked. She felt less pressure, a bit less danger, but she knew it might not be as easy or successful as it was the other time.

"Hmm…" Konstantin carefully looked at Veronika. "I actually do, very much," he finally said thoughtfully, drawing out the words. "How did you know?"

He placed the knife on the seat. Veronika relaxed a tiny bit. She knew that she still had work to do, but she remembered Mikhail.

"I, uuuh" Veronika began hesitatingly; she, of course, didn't know anything else about him or much about Kant, so she lied. "As soon as I saw you, I thought that you were so interesting, so unusual, that you should appreciate and understand somebody as complex as Kant!"

A shadow of interest flashed in the eyes of the young man. Noticing this change, Veronika quickly continued:

"I'm interested in your opinion: Did he believe in God or not?"

"Well, that is debatable." Konstantin leaned back. "You see, Kant never said that God existed, but he wrote about this idea of God based on infinity, eternity, existence outside the present world, omnipresence…"

He spoke more and more enthusiastically, but Veronika didn't really care what he was saying because he wasn't as much of a threat any more. She gradually regained her composure, and even managed to express admiration, leaning toward Konstantin, assented, and shook her head in amazement. Not really understanding the essence of his monologue, Veronika, nevertheless, skillfully inserted "What, really?" "No, seriously?" and "How interesting."

Pretending to be a grateful listener, she very carefully watched her obviously mentally ill companion and, as soon as she felt that the talk about Kant was coming to an end, inserted another topic.

"And what are your thoughts about… Spinoza?"

"Well, he actually criticized the *Bible*! And he also spoke of God as merging with nature," Konstantin said and swallowed the bait. The crazy glow in his eyes disappeared; he forgot about the knife and started reciting facts from the biographies of both philosophers enthusiastically. Veronika almost calmed down.

"The girl woke up at night, she's so uptight, and just a

bit mad, her pillow's all covered in blood," Mumiy Troll purred lusciously from the speakers. It was two a.m.

"Well," said Konstantin, "let's go. I'll take you home. You're cool, you know! Will you give me your number?"

"Sure!" Veronika assured him, overjoyed. "Write it down!"

And she gave him the same number she had long ago memorized. It was Mikhail all over again! Veronika was proud of herself and vowed to avoid things like this in the future.

***

Veronika met Anatoly where she met everyone else, at the bus stop, when she was hitching a ride to get to college. A brand-new blue Mercedes braked hard near her; the driver jumped out and gallantly opened the passenger door. As soon as she looked into his smart brown eyes behind the stylish glasses and saw his humble smile, Veronika immediately trusted him and without an ounce of concern, got into the car.

Anatoly turned out to be a great conversationalist. He entertained her all the way to her college with jokes, stories from his university years, countries he had visited, and even shared some cooking recipes. Veronika was delighted. The new acquaintance delivered her without incident and, appearing embarrassed, asked if she would give him her number. Unexpectedly, Veronika gave him her real number and caught herself thinking that she wanted him to kiss her goodbye. Anatoly did not kiss her but promised to call in the evening and to take her to school again the next morning.

They started dating. On weekdays he drove her to classes and back home, and on the weekends, they went to Saint Petersburg and visited museums, exhibitions, and parks. He was the first guy she introduced to her parents. Sasha didn't count because they had known Sasha since he was born.

Anatoly won over Veronika's mother by bringing her flowers every time he came to pick up his girlfriend. They had been dating for two weeks when he met Veronika's father—he came home from work unexpectedly early.

"Now I understand where Veronika's good looks come from." Anatoly shyly looked at Olga Nikolayevna and then turned his eyes on Nikolay Andreyevich. "And her smarts."

All four were sitting in the living room, having tea with cake covered in white puffy cream and strewn with cherries. Of course, it was Anatoly, who had brought it.

"May I be honest?" he continued and said, without waiting for an answer. "I immediately fell in love when I saw your treasure at the bus stop! And when Veronika gave me her number, I felt like I was flying and couldn't wait to call her!"

Veronika blushed. Anatoly was the man of her dreams, her Prince Charming—in a brand-new blue BMW even! He wasn't just older—at twenty-seven, he seemed to be so mature, a businessman, and an excellent boyfriend. He bought her gifts, flowers, and sweets and took her to the most expensive restaurants in Saint Petersburg. She wasn't ashamed to introduce him to her mother and father. On the contrary, Veronika was proud of him and wanted Anatoly to introduce her to his parents, his younger brother Sergei, and their German shepherd—he talked a lot about them all.

The only thing that affected Veronika's happiness was that she had a fight with her best friend. She felt Alina was actually to blame for everything that went wrong. In the early days of their relationship, Anatoly invited both of them to the sauna. His friends also gathered there. They had fun, bathed, jumped into the ice-cold pool and chatted at the table, richly laden with snacks and alcohol. The girls had wine, and the men drank vodka. Suddenly, during a lively conversation they were all having, Anatoly jumped up and slapped Alina in the face so hard that she fell on the floor. Veronika was about to rush to her friend, but Alina got up and ran out of the room, pressing her hand to her burning cheek. Anatoly held Veronika by the shoulders and explained that "that arrogant bitch" told him something very dirty and indecent, humiliating him "in front of all the homeboys," so she had to be taught a "lesson."

The next day, Alina called Veronika on the phone and said that a man who hit a woman was not a man, that she didn't want anything to do with him and wouldn't want someone like that for her friend.

"It's either me or that asshole. Your choice," concluded Alina with an ultimatum. "If you want to be with him, our friendship is over."

Veronika sighed in annoyance and hung up. She was certain that Alina was simply jealous.

She had no time to give any more serious thought to Alina's words. That evening, Anatoly invited her to his place. Veronika was nervous about meeting his parents, little brother, and the dog. She really wanted his family to like her. She put on her best dress, the checkered one, took her mother's modest jewelry, carefully drew wings on her eyes, put on some mascara, and applied soft lilac lipstick to her lips.

Having run her fingers through her hair that had flattened under the hat, Veronika buzzed Anatoly's apartment. He opened the door and gestured for her to enter. He looked amazing in jeans, a white turtleneck, and a three-day stubble. He kissed her on the lips and led her into the entryway where he helped her take off her coat. He smelled of expensive cologne.

"I'll be waiting for you in the living room," he said, smiling charmingly.

Loud techno sounds came from the room where he had gone, and Veronika was amused that Anatoly's parents were so open-minded and modern. She looked at herself critically in the mirror and noticed a pimple that was just about to emerge on her chin. She grimaced at the pimple and timidly stepped into the living room. Anatoly was sitting on the couch. There was a hookah on the table in front of him, an ashtray with still smoking cigarette butts, an almost empty bottle of vodka, and a few shot glasses.

"Oh, are you alone?" Veronika was surprised.

"Yeah," Anatoly answered casually, pouring vodka into an empty glass. "Come on, drink!"

Veronika didn't have the courage to ask whose glasses were on the table and was afraid to say no, even though she couldn't stand the taste of vodka. She drank it all in one gulp.

"Undress for me. Do it sexy, baby!" said Anatoly saucily and changed the tape in the recorder. Some kind of slow music began playing.

Veronika felt aroused and surrendered to his dominating tone. She started to spin slowly taking off her dress and pantyhose on the go.

"Come on! Take it all off."

Veronika took off her bra and panties and threw them at him, smiling.

"Hey, what the hell are you doing, slut?"

She was shocked by the way he acted, but then he ordered:

"On your knees, bitch!"

Veronika hastily got on all fours, thinking that this was probably some kind of role-play.

"I'll be right back," Anatoly said and left the room. Veronika's vision blurred from the alcohol, and her hands and bare feet filled with warmth. She thought that she wouldn't drink anything else, but she wanted a smoke. A cigarette for two... She recalled her friend Alina.

'It's a pity that Alina is jealous because of Anatoly. I can't even tell anyone besides her something like this.'

The sound of the opening door interrupted her thoughts. The lights went out in the room. In a strange, changed voice, Anatoly ordered Veronika to remain silent and not to turn around. Someone else, not him, grabbed her from behind and painfully squeezed her breasts with his cold hands. This man reeked of alcohol. She was so disgusted she felt sick.

She tried to get free, but the same cold hands squeezed her wrists this time, and a sweaty body pressed against her back.

"Spread your legs!" She heard her boyfriend's voice from the other side of the room. "Spread them, I said! And don't you dare move!"

Veronika couldn't fight him off, she couldn't even move. Tears streamed down her cheeks. From the sounds in the dark, she could hear that there were several other people in the room, besides these two. The one with sweat and cold hands began raping her from behind, moving quickly, not stopping to pause. Someone else grabbed her by the neck and poured vodka into her mouth, which burned her throat and it felt like everything inside, too. Someone turned up the music to the max. The rapist was still going, pressing on her with his enormous weight, so that Veronika had difficulty breathing. Her head was spinning from vodka, pain, humiliation, and an overwhelming sense of degradation and powerlessness. Someone lit a cigarette, and in that light, she saw the face of Anatoly's friend. He had been in the sauna with them that one time. Next to him she could make out, it seemed, more familiar faces, but she felt so sick that she almost stopped comprehending. With head hunched over, she hung helplessly in the hands of the rapist. Tears wouldn't stop running down her face, and she felt how salty and warm they were. Finally, the sweaty man pulled away, but another one replaced him, and then a third and a fourth. She lost count, and then she lost consciousness.

***

Veronika didn't say anything to anyone and didn't go to the police. She recalled with horror how she became conscious, lying naked on the floor, when someone squirted some water on her.

"If you go to the police or tell anyone, I'll find you and

kill you—and your parents," said her former lover. "Understand? That'll be all; you're free to go!"

Veronika ran into Sasha at the pharmacy two months after that hideous 'party'. Almost all this time she had stayed at home in bed; only sometimes she would appear at college, moving like a pale shadow. Studying made no sense. Veronika didn't know how to keep on living. She didn't want to go anywhere, didn't want to see anyone or speak to anyone—so that there would be no talk, no questions. She suffered from insomnia and wanted only to fall asleep, to not remember anything or, even better, to disappear, to die. To die from cruel deception, betrayal, from unbearable shame and disappointment in people, in the whole world, but mostly in herself.

How? How could he do this to her? He was so... it was hard for her to look back at how he was before that last meeting. She tied herself in knots with the endless "whys." Why did he do it? Why did he do this to her? Why to her?

One time she even thought about telling Alina about this whole nightmare. After all, she was her only close friend. Almost immediately, she dismissed this idea: no, she couldn't go to Alina because she had warned Veronika to stay away from that "sorry excuse of a man."

She just couldn't get her head around what had happened. She was eighteen, still childish in some respects, and couldn't even imagine that she had simply become the victim of a psychopath—a manipulator, a rapist, and a sadist.

***

"A unique offer! A pill that will give you instant happiness!" said Sasha in a singsong voice, mimicking the detergent commercial. "Wanna try? You'll love it!"

Veronika watched water vapors coming from his mouth as he spoke and then melting against the bright blue sky. They were standing at the edge of the forest, where snow still lay in piles among the naked birches. Cold, Veronika snuggled up to Sasha, kissed him on the lips, and took the pill from his hands.

"And what will happen?" she asked, examining the white round tablet in her palm.

"Everything will be fantastic, my little one!" Sasha laughed, pressed Veronika against his chest, and kissed her.

For the first time in many days, she was laughing again, and it was so good to be with him. Veronika put the pill in her mouth and swallowed.

After a few minutes, she felt peace descend upon her. Her hands and feet warmed up, and she felt easy in her mind. It was all so clear, so light. She was filled from the inside with something resembling all-consuming, universal love… Mom's image came to Veronika, Mom that she never knew: a happy and loving mother was waiting for her at home, cooked a whole bowl of pies, and there was meatball soup on the stove...

It seemed to Veronika that she could smell the food, only now, she didn't want to eat; she didn't want anything at all, she just felt so good. With a blissful smile, she looked at the black-and-white tree trunks that somehow looked like fairy-tale gnomes in strange hats. They looked back at her kindly and called out to her. Leaves suddenly blossomed on the birches, gradually turning a neon green, and the sky was now a pale pink hue. The forest no longer seemed scary but was magical and mysteriously enticing.

"I feel so good when I'm with you, Sa-asha…"

He hugged her and breathed in her warmth.

"I love you, Veronika."

"I love you too, Sasha."

***

He didn't ask her why she had disappeared more than a year ago. When he discovered the money from his cache was gone, Sasha immediately guessed that Veronika had stolen it. But either because for him the amount was not significant, or because he loved Veronika, he didn't hold grudges. He was not going to confront her. He even somehow understood her motivations and justified her actions. He quickly forgave her. And now he was happy that she was back. It felt good being with her.

Together, they continued to take these "pills of happiness," and Veronika made love with him in a way that he couldn't even imagine in his teenage fantasies. She moaned and screamed with pleasure, and he looked at her and almost went crazy with love.

He could no longer sneak these pills from his grandmother's medicine—the shortage was becoming too evident. Through his friends, though, he found a "contact" who supplied them without fail. Veronika was grateful to him for this: the "pills" for some time eased the painful memories and dulled the feeling of fear, which firmly stuck with her after the rape.

Every day, she woke up and every night, she fell asleep,

51

thinking about what had happened to her and why. Could this be punishment for her sins? After all, she had taken advantage of Sasha's trust and stolen from him. And she became an accomplice in the robbery of that food kiosk. She thought about Ivan and Pavel-the-Orphan, who had talked her and Alina into that crime. The police found the boys; they were tried and sent to prison. And how low it was to steal make-up for sale from Azamat and Amid!

Or maybe Anatoly did this to her because she... she was really a slut? After all, she got into the car with Mikhail and two more men, and agreed to go with Konstantin, who turned out to be a maniac... And how many times she jumped into cars with strangers without even thinking just so they would give her a ride for free... And, probably, her mother screamed at her and called her a slut for a reason when Veronika came home late... Slut...

'That doctor, that gynecologist was also right,' Veronika thought now, recalling how she had shocked the woman, saying that she didn't know how many men she had slept with. 'She's an experienced doctor, she knows.' Yes, Veronika was brutally raped and that encounter also gave her gonorrhea... and she really didn't know how many 'partners' she had had... then... But it was she who was raped! So, is it she and only she who is to blame for everything?

'Perhaps, this is karma,' she concluded with despair and sadness.

All these confused thoughts and emotional pain were dulled only with the help of the pills that Sasha got for her. Veronika began her mornings by imagining how she and Sasha would "dose up" later, and everything would be fine.

The pills made it all go away, and completely different thoughts came to her—about anything else, but not about what had happened to her. Finally... Veronika felt like she used to before all that horror.

She hurried to get ready for dates, most often to Sasha's grandparents' apartment, the very one that she and Alina had broken into, and could hardly wait for Sasha to give her the daily dose.

Veronika soon started dropping by not only after classes but also before, and Sasha started to call his 'contact' daily. She didn't even notice how all the painful thoughts about what had happened to her were replaced by repetitive thoughts about the pills.

'I need to see Sasha before classes,' she told herself, barely opening her eyes in the morning, and began getting ready in a hurry. 'Everything is fine, everything's just fine. I just need to take one pill. A quick shower first, then I get dressed, and off to Sasha I go.'

"Breakfast? No, I can't! I'm late for school!" Veronika would shout to her mother, already in the hallway, hand on the doorknob, while she thought only of one thing: 'I need to take a pill right now and breakfast—well, maybe later... Take a pill, take a pill, take a pill... Damn, I think I forgot that report on... What was it? I don't remember... doesn't matter.... I need a pill... First. I'll take it, then I'll think about everything else.'

Those were the only thoughts popping up in her head while she drove to Sasha's place. By the time she got to college, she was already high.

Returning from class, Veronika felt happy. 'It's so fortunate that I was smart enough to grab a pill for the evening... I'll come home, take it and feel better right away... or maybe I should... just take it right now?'

Gradually, her entire life seemed to have become all about this one incessant thing: pills. Veronika had completely lost control over her thought process.

She remembered well the day when Sasha didn't answer her call. As she was holding the phone, she noticed that her hands were shaking. 'What the hell is this?' thought Veronika, but the pills were more important so she returned to the call. She dialed Sasha's number again and again until she heard some girl's voice on the other end.

"Hello?"

"Who is this?" Veronika got very confused and immediately asked in a raspy voice. "Can I speak to Sasha?"

"No! Sasha's busy! With me!" said the impudent stranger and hung up.

There was a click. The connection was lost, then short beeps followed. Her hands couldn't stop shaking.

'What can I do? What should I do?' Veronika tried to find a solution. The shakes got worse. She felt sick. Exhausted, she sat on her bed. Her stomach hurt badly. Veronika was certain that this wasn't a virus. 'But what is it with me?' The brain again and again kept saying: Pills. Take one, and everything will be fine.

She needed to go see Sasha... Veronika forced herself to get up from the bed, put on her coat, grab the keys and run out of the apartment. As soon as she had gotten to the bus stop and waved her hand, a car stopped in front of her.

"Can you please take me to 11 Lenin Street, for free? Pretty please!"

Veronika was shaking, and the driver, an obese gray-haired man of about fifty-five, look at her with suspicion and caution.

"Are you sick or something?"

"No. Will you give me a ride? Please! I really need to get there!"

"Not for free, I won't. But if you return the favor, then you are welcome!"

The driver pushed open the passenger door from the inside and with a welcoming gesture pointed Veronika to the seat.

She got inside. Shivering, barely uttering the words, she asked, "Could you turn on the heat?"

"Sure!" the driver answered exaggeratedly politely and pressed a button on the heater. Veronika began to warm up little by little although her hands were still freezing and shaking. She stared blankly in front of her, words spinning chaotically in her head.

'Pills… need to get to Sasha… Who was that girl that picked up the phone? Why is she with him? What's happening to me? Am I sick? I just need a pill, just one… one… pill… And Sasha's, probably home…'

That last thought calmed her down a bit, and Veronika briefly blanked out. She came to herself when she heard the driver's voice who seemed to be asking her something.

"Sorry?"

"I asked you, do you like the 'boatman' song?" the driver turned on the stereo.

"What? Oh, yes, of course, thanks."

Veronika had no idea what she was being asked about, but at that moment, she didn't care. She stared out the window.

'And then I took the man by the shoulder and said quietly, I'll kill you, boatman!' the driver turned up the music to the full. Veronika almost jumped up from surprise and instantly came to her senses. 'I will kill you, bo-atman!' roared Professor Lebedinsky.

She squeezed her hands tightly to try and calm her shakes.

"Hey, how are you feeling there?" the driver turned off the engine. "We're here!"

"I'm fine." She found speaking difficult, nearly impossible.

"Then it's time to return the favor. Come on!"

He unzipped his fly, looked guardedly around to make sure they were alone, then grabbed Veronika by the neck and pushed her down. Immediately, she felt nauseated and could not help but throw up on his pants.

"What are you doing, whore?" the man shouted and pushed her away.

Veronika continued uncontrollably vomiting on the floor.

"Stupid slut! Filthy junkie! Get the hell out of here!"

Veronika didn't remember how she got out of the car. Her head was pounding, and she couldn't think. Staggering, she barely made it to Sasha's entrance and somehow made it to the fifth floor. It felt like it took her ages to get there. She rang the doorbell for a long time and knocked on the door, but no one opened. Veronika's body started to shake, as if from a fever, and she limply slid back against the wall on the dirty floor. She was writhing, everything was aching—every muscle, every bone, every joint. 'My God? What is it? Withdrawal? But I didn't inject myself with anything! I'm not a junkie!'

Her panic thoughts were interrupted by the neighbor. The same man, who caught her and Alina a year ago, when they were trying to open the door to Sasha's apartment. Apparently, he still thought that she lived here.

"Are you feeling sick? Can't open the door again? Nobody's home?" the old man was concerned.

Sweat dripped into Veronika's eyes, down her back, and she was both cold and hot. She could barely breathe from all that pain but managed to whisper, "Please, call an ambulance…"

***

In the hospital, Veronika started feeling better only on the sixth day. She couldn't even get out of bed. To ease her withdrawal symptoms, she was given methadone. Upon discharge, the doctors warned her that after the physical withdrawal was over, the psychological would begin. They advised her to look for a group of Drug Addicts Anonymous. Veronika was skeptical: she didn't consider herself a drug addict.

From the hospital she went straight home. As she aneared her neighborhood, she suddenly felt an urge to call Sasha. She immediately checked herself.

'Call Sasha… and what? Ask for pills?'

'Yes,' replied a strange voice in her head ahead of her own thoughts. 'You ask him for only one pill just to pull yourself together, and, at the same time, you find out who that bitch was at his place.'

Veronika slowed down.

'Go straight to him,' insisted the voice in her head. 'Go to Sasha… his house is in the opposite direction.'

Veronika stopped and looked around in dismay, as if not recognizing the buildings around. And then a sign caught her eye on the corner of the nearest house: Narcotics Anonymous. Come Join Us.

'Maybe it's an omen.' Veronika's heart began pounding, and she darted to the door under the sign.

A steep narrow staircase led into the basement. Veronika carefully walked down and almost immediately saw a group of people. They sat in a circle and listened to a girl, who was saying something and crying. Noticing Veronika, she stopped and looked inquiringly at the man who, apparently, was in charge of this gathering.

"Hello, come in, take a free chair, and welcome!" he said to Veronika amiably. "My name is Alexey. I am the leading specialist at the center."

He had an oval face with delicate features, a genuine warm smile, and deep brown eyes.

Veronika sat in the circle and looked around. There were about a dozen men and women of different ages. Some greeted her quietly, nodding their heads, and the girls next to her introduced themselves, "Yulia. Marina."

"So, Alena, please, tell us what made you start doing drugs?" Alexey adjusted his glasses and turned to the sad-looking pale girl that sat in front of Veronika.

"I don't know. I just felt bad, I felt bad all over and hurt. The heroin helped me forget about everything that had happened to me, and then I was too deep into it and got used to it," said Alena.

"Can you tell us what's happened to you?"

"I lost a child and my fiancée, then my work, my livelihood... I lost everything and ended up on the street. At the very bottom. Everything happened so suddenly—that accident, the call..."

The girl cried. Everyone in the room was silent.

"Go on, we're listening to you, and we are here with you," Alexey encouraged her.

He himself had stopped using heroin five years ago. He got hooked on drugs after the death of his mother, whom he loved very much and to whom he was very close. When she was diagnosed with brain cancer, she didn't have much time left. She withered away in just a couple of months. Alexey was with her all the time, taking care of her until the very end. His father had died of a heart attack even earlier. So, when his mother passed, Alexey felt so low that he asked a stranger, a junkie at the train station, to inject him. He hadn't tried drugs before. He knew, of course, that they could help him forget about everything, including his pain. He spent five months injecting almost constantly after that first time, in a daze and half-conscious. When he awoke once in the hospital after an overdose, he realized that he was in a trap.

Centers for Narcotics Anonymous were just starting to open in Russia, and Alexey went to one of them in Saint Petersburg. A few years later, he was still attending these meetings, and this is when he created the first Narcotics Anonymous branch in the town where he lived.

"When my family died in a car accident," Alena continued, "I just blew off work. Friends, happiness, money, I didn't even care. This mental hell went on... I don't know how long. I don't even remember anymore how or when I started shooting up, but six years have passed since then."

"You are now here with us," Alexey said. "You've found a way to break free from your addiction. Heroin didn't help you."

"Yes, you're right. Heroin helped only while it was working. I escaped from the reality."

"And now you're back. This is life. This is reality. You want to continue living, right?" asked Alexey.

"Yes. I want to live."

"You still have your whole life ahead of you. You can have a new, different life, love, and family, if you want it. You must decide for yourself—live or use heroin again. It can't be both. If you choose to live, then we are with you, and we will help you."

Alexey again adjusted his glasses and turned to the newcomer.

"What brought you to us? Ready to share? Or you want to wait for the next time?"

"I was… raped…" said Veronika, looking at her clenched fists, as tears streamed down her face. "I could not tell anyone about this. My best friend won't talk to me and my boyfriend, who hooked me on pills, is now seeing some other girl!"

"If you don't mind, let's get on a first-name basis. What's your name?"

"Veronika."

"Very nice to meet you, Veronika," said Alexey in a soothing voice. "Do you want to share something else?"

"Yes!" she cried out desperately, "I'm a slut…" She continued her sobbing.

"Veronika, can you hear me? We've got you. We're with you."

***

Sasha didn't expect that he would be so hurt by this whole thing. Veronika called him that day, and that dummy Ksenia, his classmate, grabbed the phone while he was in the shower and basically told her to go to hell.

He was angry at Ksenia at first, but then he remembered that she didn't make him sleep with her. He was just as guilty: got carried away, seduced her. The affair didn't last long, Sasha was with her just a couple of times and only when he was under the influence of drugs. The passion died down just as quickly as the high, but still, it had happened.

He wished he could fix everything. He kept calling Veronika but could not reach her. He went to her house, but whoever was there kept telling him that Veronika wasn't home and would be back late. Realizing that all his attempts were futile, Sasha got deeper into drugs. He hardly noticed anymore with whom he was spending his nights: was it Kseniya? Kristina? Maybe Olesya? It didn't matter. Any one of them would do. On one of those bad days Sasha survived an overdose. He ended up in the hospital, but immediately after being discharged, he called his "contact" again. He could not stop the cycle of wanting to quit and being unable to.

Sasha's father found out about his drug addiction, but instead of sending his son to treatment and rehabilitation or at least locking him in at home, he stopped giving him money. Sasha feverishly started thinking up ways of getting his next dose. He urgently needed cash, otherwise—he already knew this from his past experience—he would have unbearable withdrawals. The decision came to him unexpectedly. Recalling an episode from a television series that his grandmother liked to watch, Sasha broke into a car that was parked in the next neighborhood, pulled out all the expensive equipment from it, and sold it to a pawnshop. Just enough for a shot... The police found him at home the very next day—he hadn't even thought about hiding.

He spent half a year in prison. Those horrifying six months dragged out like a nonstop nightmare. He thought he had died and gone to hell. He was beaten up and abused. He dreamed of freedom. But when he got out, he had nowhere to go: his very old-school grandparents wanted nothing to do with a grandson who had served time. He was out of jail, but he did not know where to go or what to do. He wandered around the city for a long time. Cold, hungry, no money in his pocket, he decided to go see Veronika. Her grandmother, Arina Andreyevna, opened the door. Veronika was not home. Unexpectedly for him, Sasha, hiding his face, asked to borrow some money. He said that he had been in prison and was just released, that he was kicked out of his grandparents' house and had nothing to live on.

The old, grey-haired woman, who knew Sasha's family, sighed, shook her head, and thanked God that Veronika no longer spoke to Sasha. But she couldn't deny money to her friends' grandson, so she gave him a little for food. Arina Andreyevna didn't call Sasha's grandmother. She didn't say anything to her husband, either: Veronika's grandfather had high blood pressure, and she was afraid that he would take it too hard. He wasn't allowed to worry. Of course, she also said nothing to Veronika.

***

Sasha stepped out of the building and took out the creased bills from his pocket. It wasn't enough for pills, just for an injection. Having forgotten that he was going to buy food, he went straight to the train station, where, he knew for sure, drug dealers were hanging out.

In the stall of a reeking bathroom, he awkwardly stuck the syringe into his vein, stumbled out, got to the nearest nook, sat on the dirty floor, and passed out.

Sasha woke up in the hospital. He barely remembered what happened after that—only IV drips, drips, more drips, and the grey ragged ceiling...

The meetings in Narcotics Anonymous, where Sasha went on his doctor's advice, didn't help much. Still, he realized that he needed to run as far as possible from his usual environment. His father—Sasha managed to find him and swore that this was the last time he was asking for a favor—agreed to help. He sent his son to the Czech Republic, to the Břevnov Monastery. Together with the monks, Sasha got up at four in the morning and went to bed at eight in the evening. During the day, he exhausted himself with work and prayers to God, that he didn't believe.

***

Sometimes Veronika dialed Sasha's number out of habit. Hearing the voice of his grandparents, she hung up. Every day, she diligently attended the Narcotics Anonymous meetings. She liked the people in the group, and she felt sympathy for every one of them. She had heard about such groups before, but for some reason, she thought she would see vicious criminals there, who would offer her drugs. When she got to know them better, she realized that they were deeply unhappy people, abandoned by their parents or loved ones, or they had lost someone. The grief, pain, or abuse that they were unable to handle on their own made them try heroin or something else. Despite their own problems, the people in the group were considerate and sensitive to others' suffering and very supportive of one another.

"My mother doesn't love me, and my father doesn't love me, either. They left me here and moved to America," Veronika once said in the heat of the moment at a meeting.

All sixteen people in the room were silent. There was both interest and empathy in their eyes. They just didn't know what to say.

The first to respond was the kindly looking girl with dark circles under her eyes.

"Did your parents leave you all alone and head to America?"

"Well, not really. I live with my grandparents. I still needed to finish college when my parents left."

"Come on, don't blame it all on your folks," a fair, curly-haired young guy smiled broadly. "They didn't leave you. They probably wanted you to get your college degree and are waiting for you there." Then he frowned and said, "Mine were drunks and died one after another, and I will never see them again. I have no one else, no grandparents, no sisters, no brothers, no aunts, no uncles, no one!"

Veronika felt ashamed. Before this guy confessed that he was left completely alone in this world, she didn't think how important it was that she wasn't an orphan and had a grandmother and a grandfather here. And her parents really couldn't wait to see her. Veronika knew this, and she knew that she was the one who had not wanted to leave with them.

After the meeting, Alexey approached her.

"Veronika," he said, "you have already come to enough of these meetings, so I can ask you. Do you understand what is the most important thing for a drug addict on the way to freedom? How can you attempt to get rid of addiction easier and completely? What should you change?"

"The social circle, place of residence, and things that are associated with use," Veronika rapped out.

"Exactly! Only I will tell you one secret: the most important thing is to change the place. The environment and associations change with the place—everything does! And the farther away, the better. Do you see what I mean?"

"Uh... no..." she looked at him from under her puckered brows.

"Come on, Veronika!" eagerly exclaimed Alexey. "You have this amazing opportunity to go to America and not just temporarily change your location, but completely change everything: your place of residence and, accordingly, your environment! Everything!" Alexey deliberately stressed every word. "Everything that connects you with your addiction. You will begin a new life there, and your obsessive thinking about drugs will gradually go away by itself and be replaced by thoughts about what is happening in your new life. This is your chance, Veronika! Don't miss it!"

Veronika finally understood the meaning of his words, and when she did, it took her breath away. America, the place of her dreams! Maybe it really could be her salvation.

When Veronika told the group that she had stayed because of college, she wasn't entirely telling the truth. Her parents were trying to persuade her to go with them and finish her studies at an American school.

Veronika had dreamed of America since she was little. The country of Hollywood stars and the birthplace of her idols—Marilyn Monroe, Madonna, Michael Jackson—a fairy-tale version of America, where everything seemed possible.

The older she got, the more she noticed the stagnation, wretchedness and the poverty in which she was born and was growing up. She was more and more depressed by the ill-being, social exclusion, injustice, all the angry, unhappy people around, and her own parents, who were living from paycheck to paycheck.

She remembered her whole life how her mother yelled at her father when he ate the orange that she had left "for the child." Veronika felt sorry for her father and at the same time, ashamed, because she was that child for whom the stupid fruit was intended. Since then, Veronika hated oranges.

Or, one day, her mother made a scene because Veronika accidentally spilled flour on the floor. How she was screaming then…

"Oh, you clumsy idiot! You can't help with anything; you only make it worse! Now you and your father will stay hungry! They won't give us another coupon!"

Veronika didn't understand what coupons were, but she knew that without them, people couldn't buy flour, sugar, butter, meat or even bread. Flour was the most important product: homemade pies with potatoes, cabbage, mushrooms, and eggs were very filling—the whole family could go for several days. Sugar almost all went to jams. They prepared a lot at home, for the whole year, and in winter it replaced fresh fruits, which were also in short supply in summer.

Once, her mother came home exhausted after a hard day at work, fell on the couch in the living room and sent eight-year-old Veronika to the grocery store. She slipped her some money and those coupons and gave her scrupulous instructions. "One bottle of milk! Before crossing the road, be sure to look right and left! Better go with the other women."

Veronika had to walk to the grocery store through their neighborhood, then through the next, then through a busy street, and then another block. It was a huge distance for a little girl. She remembered well that grocery line, stretching to the store for two and sometimes even three blocks. The annoyed, hostile crowd was ready to break out for any reason, and it terrified Veronika. Frightened by just the sight of the large overbearing women, yelling at one another, "You didn't stand here! Move!" she quietly stood at the edge and was worried all the time that they would push her, squeeze her out, or even throw her out.

And so it happened that day. Veronika waited in line for an hour and a half and was standing at the very entrance to the store when a tall overweight woman jumped up to her and obnoxiously screamed, "Get out of here—you weren't standing here!" She shoved Veronika and took her place.

Veronika was confused. She felt scared, hurt, and ashamed. Shrinking, she took a couple of steps back. People in the line who saw it stood with stone faces or looked away, pretending that nothing had happened. She cried and ran home. She was upset by such treatment, and her mother's anticipated reaction was even more frightening. Mother would certainly yell at her or, worse, cry when she learned that her daughter had returned with nothing.

Veronika was rushing home with an empty milk bottle and an annoyingly rattling lid, thinking of all the possible consequences and choking with tears, when she heard the overwhelmingly loud screech of the tires. A car stopped abruptly right next to her. She didn't notice that she had run out onto the road at the red light. She froze in the middle of the roadway, her tears instantly dried up.

"Stu-u-u-pid fucking bitch! Watch where the fuck you're going, idiot!" The driver looked out the car window and cursed.

Some elderly man ran to the girl, grabbed her hand, and led her off the road to the sidewalk. The driver drove off immediately, and Veronika gratefully looked at her rescuer, even though he shook his head in dismay and waggled his finger before leaving.

Her mother didn't want to hear anything about the line, the woman, or the car. She just yelled frantically that now she couldn't cook milk soup, and the whole family would be left without food because "her idiot of a daughter couldn't buy a bottle of milk."

Veronika hid in the corner of her bed. Eyes filled with tears and very hungry, she fell asleep. Since that day, she felt sick even when someone simply mentioned milk.

Her mother scolded her often, and Veronika never actually knew what she would get in trouble for. Once she got yelled at for the transparent plastic bag from under the cottage cheese or something that she threw into the garbage. These damn bags had to be washed thoroughly with soap, dried by hanging them up, and then carefully folded and put into the kitchen cabinet to be reused.

"Loser!" her mother was raging in the heat of the moment when her father hadn't received his salary again. "You are a useless moron! If you don't bring money home, what will we be living on? Did you think about that? Have you thought about us? Do you even think of anything besides your stupid work, for which you don't get paid!"

Little Veronika felt terribly sorry for her father. She was certain that he was to blame for nothing. He spent day and night at his institute, and his salary was held back just like the others'. However, she also felt sorry for her mother even though she constantly yelled at both of them. At ten, Veronika already understood that her mother behaved like that because she was having the hardest time of all.

In the ninth grade, secretly, she went to Saint Maria's Church on Vasilyevsky Island in Saint Petersburg. She heard from someone that if you left a note with a wish on the wall of the temple, it would certainly come true.

"I don't want to live like this; I don't want to live here; I want to live in America, where all dreams come true," Veronika wrote on a piece of paper, rolled it up and put it into a crack. Back then, her parents were nowhere near going to America. Veronika couldn't even hope for that to happen. She never told anyone about that dream of hers.

That her father was invited to work in the States was a real shock to everyone. It was completely unexpected, rare, extraordinary luck! And it plunged the whole family into a state of disbelief, which was soon replaced by a worrisome excitement because now they had to pack and prepare.

Veronika really wanted to go with her parents. Of course, she did! She was one step away from a dream come true! Her mother, who had suddenly become noticeably cheerful and even started to look younger, volunteered to go to Veronika's college to withdraw her.

However, at the last moment, Veronika, hiding her sadness, firmly said to her, "I won't be coming with you. I need to graduate from college and then I'm going to the university. I will be staying with my grandparents."

Her mother was surprised, but didn't insist, she was so sick and tired of everything that she wanted to leave as soon as possible. Her father, as always, said nothing, and most likely, his thoughts were filled with nuclear reactors. Her conservative grandparents were happy that their granddaughter had decided to stay and finish her education in her home country. Nobody knew the true reason why Veronika refused to go. She didn't even realize it until much later.

Shortly before her father was invited to America was when Veronika got hooked on pills. She was deceiving herself with ideas that she needed to graduate from college and, possibly, the university, and only then go to the States. She no longer controlled herself at that point, and her addiction decided for her. The voice in her head whispered gloatingly, "When your parents leave, you will have complete freedom. You feel good here. You can't go."

If only she had understood then that she practically had no freedom left, that she had become obsessed with drugs.

Her parents packed their few things, sold their small one-bedroom apartment, and with tears in their eyes, but happy and full of new hope left for Atlanta, Georgia. Veronika stayed. Almost every day, her grandfather brought printed emails from her parents from his workplace, and the three of them read aloud how her mother and father had settled in there. Her mother called on Saturdays, and her voice sounded happy and satisfied like never before. Veronika couldn't believe her ears. Her mother had changed so much: she oozed confidence, calmness, joy, and she was content with her life. She excitedly talked about their large and sunny apartment, the brand-new Ford Taurus (their first car!), how they both were learning to drive, that she took English as a Second Language classes, and that her father was working all the time just like he always did. She talked about their neighbors, their new pets, a red cat named Peaches and Marsik, a pit bull. Listening to this, Veronika, who always dreamed of having a dog or at least a cat, recalled how her mother always harshly denied her pleas for a pet: "I don't even have enough money to feed you and your father. How can you even think about a cat or a dog?"

Veronika remembered how much she resented her mother. And now... She was not at all interested in her parents and their new life; she didn't care about anything at all. Except pills. Pills had her firmly in their grip. Her thoughts and will were their slaves. Veronika didn't know that the 'pills' she was taking were heroin. Like many, she didn't think that this heavy, synthesized drug and the seemingly harmless-looking pills that 'gave instant happiness' were one and the same.

**

After spending three months at the Břevnov Monastery, Sasha returned to his hometown. As soon as he got off the train, he found a seller at the station, whose face seemed familiar.

"Man, I need to get a fix."

"Come with me," the Uzbek looked around and waved his head in the direction of the restroom that was nearby. Sasha followed him. Familiar stalls, stinking of urine. Gray powder, rolled up sleeve, shining point of a needle. And then—oblivion.

**

"Sign here and here!" a young nurse in a washed-out gray coat offhandedly passed some forms to Sasha.

Before that, she casually informed him that his blood test came back positive for an HIV infection. Sasha was sitting on the edge of the bed. He didn't remember how he ended up in the hospital after the station. And now, he could hardly understand what he had just heard.

The nurse was writing something down in a notebook with a chewed ballpoint pen. She was chomping on her gum and didn't even look at Sasha.

"What is it?" he asked the nurse.

The nurse looked up from the papers and stared at the patient in surprise, apparently not expecting any questions from him.

"This is an acknowledgement form, saying that you are aware of your HIV infection and will inform your sex partners. And that you had a consultation."

"But I didn't have a consultation," Sasha said through his teeth, staring back at her.

The nurse threw a puzzled look at him, dropped the papers on his bed, and left the room. Sasha lay down on his bed and began looking at the ceiling.

About two hours later, a doctor entered his room. He had gray hair and seemed firm. He looked gravely at the patient and cleared his throat.

"Young man," he said in a formal tone, "according to your tests, including the follow-ups, you have been diagnosed with HIV. You need urgent treatment. I made an appointment with a specialist and prescribed you some medications for the first month. Here is a document, obliging you to warn your partners about your illness, and another one, that you are being discharged from our department today. Please, sign. And contact Narcotics Anonymous," he finished in a much gentler voice and then dictated the address.

United States

Veronika moved to the United States to her parents a month after the conversation with Alexey. The leader of Narcotics Anonymous managed to convince her that America was the key to her recovery. She kept replaying his words in her head for several days until she finally admitted that her chances of escaping her addiction here, by herself, even with the help of her new friends in the group, were too slim. She made up her mind and, not caring much how her parents would react to such a drastic change, at the first opportunity shared with her mother all she felt: how terribly lonely she was, how much she missed her and her father, how much she wanted to see them, and how she wanted to move to the USA and start a new a life.

"But you didn't want to come with us, my darling," her mother's voice sounded confused. "You were going to graduate from the university…"

"No, Mother! I wanted to finish college and then go to the university. And now I realize that I don't like studying here. Economics is not for me at all! You yourself said then that I could get my degree in America, and it would be better for me if I wanted to continue living there," Veronika continued pouring out her arguments, amazed at how convincing she could be.

"What about your friends? And your grandparents?"

"I don't have any friends, Mother! I told you already!"

Veronika cried out in frustration. "Alina stopped talking to me, Sasha, too. And my grandparents will support my every decision."

The grandparents did support her. They gave her a going away present, a small suitcase, and all of Veronika's modest belongings easily fit in it. Her parents bought her a plane ticket. Of course, the unknown terrified Veronika. And yet, anticipating such big changes, inspired by hopes for a brighter future, she beamed with joy and counted the days before her departure, marking them off in the calendar with a red marker.

Her beloved grandparents were sending her off at the Pulkovo Airport. They cried, hugged, and kissed their granddaughter, asked her not to forget about them and come see them as often as she can.

'My darling grandparents, they're so old, weak, and hunched over.' Veronika thought of them fondly. Part of her didn't want to leave them, while another part of her rejoiced and sang. In the pre-flight hustle and bustle, she caught herself thinking that she hadn't remembered about the pills for several hours. Veronika stopped, closed her eyes and imagined she opened wide the doors of a prison and went out to her freedom, toward the bright sunlight, toward something immense, great, and free. She confidently stretched out her hands to it. She took a deep breath and smiled happily.

***

This was Veronika's first time on an airplane. The twelve-hour flight with layovers didn't tire her at all; on the contrary, she was excited to meet her parents and see the country that she had dreamt about so much. The memories of the past and of the pills seemed to fade and wear off, replaced by new images: the people on the plane, the view of the sky and the clouds, the two-hour transfer in Frankfurt, and most important, the feeling of liberation she experienced at the airport.

'I'm no longer in that mind prison. I got out of addiction,' she told herself quietly. When Veronika got off the ramp at the Hartsfield-Jackson International Airport, she felt completely free.

Her parents, Atlanta, and state of Georgia welcomed her with open arms. Even at the airport, Veronika felt that she was in a totally different world. She couldn't stop marveling at what she was seeing around. Every single thing was amazing and new to her. All the smiling, friendly faces! The wide and smooth roads! All the nice houses, buried in green, and an incredible number of strange plants and flowers! Everything was so bright, beautiful and so different!

Her mother, her previously bitter and constantly moody mother, was behind the wheel of a shiny Ford Taurus. She was happy and calm and confident. Her father, whom Veronika hardly ever saw before because of his work, sat in the back seat with her and wanted to know everything about his daughter.

They drove to a brand-new apartment complex, where her parents had settled. Veronika, with her mouth agape, wandered around the huge three-room apartment—clean and bright, furnished with new furniture. For some time, she stared at a big tray of fruit on the table in the living room.

And she had her own room. Her own… separate… room! With a king size bed, a table and a enormous wardrobe. She fell in love with Marsik at first sight; he was such a nice, funny pittie! And, oh, that not-fat-but-big-muscled and important-looking cat: really a peach, named so!

The next day, in the morning, her mother took her to the supermarket, where anything that she ever wanted could be bought, or maybe even more. Veronika's head was spinning from all this splendor, from this incredible abundance, the extraordinary, inconceivable expanse of things to buy. When in the evening they went to the pool, which was in their own apartment complex, she was utterly flabbergasted.

'Oh my God, my God, my God,' she kept repeating to herself, not believing her luck. 'I'm in America! My dream came true. Just like I wanted!'

***

Sasha didn't know for sure where he got HIV: in prison or through a needle, but he knew that he absolutely wanted to live. He again turned to his father, saying that this was the last thing he would ask of him.

"I thought last time was the last one," snapped his father.

Sasha didn't back down.

"I need surgery."

He told him about an experimental semi-legal operation that they performed at the Institute of Human Brain. Sasha was warned that after the operation he would have no desire: along with the craving for drugs, his appetite, sex drive and even the simple desire for intimacy would disappear. Sasha was ready for anything, just to end his torture of addiction. His father agreed to allow Sasha to get the treatment.

As they explained to him, such brain surgeries were performed under local anesthesia, that is, the patient must be conscious. During surgery Sasha would have to answer the surgeon's questions about his physical sensations so that the doctor could know which part of the brain was being affected at the moment.

"For example," the attending physician patiently explained to him, "if you touch the part of the brain that controls vision, a person blinks involuntarily. When we get to the part we need, which is responsible for desires and pleasure, we will freeze it."

Sasha's surgery went on for several hours and he withstood it stoically: the local anesthesia didn't relieve the excruciating pain and the tormenting sound of the surgical saw, which they used to open his skull.

"Everything went well," said the doctor to Sasha and his father after the operation. "And now, young man," the doctor turned to Sasha, "you need to get away from here as soon as possible so that your brain can no longer return to the old associations of heroin use."

"It's the same as they told me at Narcotics Anonymous. I need to leave," Sasha thought and, afraid to look at his father, he stared at the floor and said, "Dad, please send me to United States. I need to get very far away. The doctors know what they're saying..."

But Sasha didn't go to America because he wasn't granted a visa. Even his father's connections in high places couldn't help. All that he could do for his son was to buy him an apartment in Sochi and a plane ticket.

Sochi! Bright sun, warm sea, distant beautiful mountains. And a green city. He liked to just sit on the hot golden pebbles and look at the sea. Sometimes he walked along the beach, met beautiful girls in bikinis, drank juice with them and played volleyball. He went water skiing and learned to dive. Neither a half-naked female body nor extreme entertainment evoked any emotions in him, though, or aroused any desires. It felt as if there were no wants, no cravings left in his brain.

'I'm probably completely recovered already,' thought Sasha, sitting in a cafe on the promenade and unenthusiastically picking on seafood that he used to love, but which now only made him nauseous. He deliberately forced himself to remember about the drugs, but the thought didn't go beyond his command, as if falling from a cliff.

***

Veronika loved to swim in the pool and spent all her free time in it. She was pleased and even flattered that the American neighbors, who came to swim there too, tried their best to communicate with her despite the language barrier. The neighbors were very open and friendly and constantly had picnics, where they grilled meat and vegetables and invited her to join.

At one of these parties, she met Todd. He openly eyed her from head to foot, and then he winked and made a funny face.

Veronika didn't understand everything he said but was

fascinated by his bright blue eyes, dirty blond curls, full lips, and wide smile. Todd joked and laughed, imitating Veronika's strong Russian accent and mimicking famous actors. He himself looked like a character from an American movie. Veronika admitted to herself, while not knowing how to feel about this, that Todd also reminded her of Sasha—not only by his looks, but also by behavior and personality traits. She felt that she was falling for him.

On the very first night of their romance, they were caught.

"What's going on here?" a police flashlight lit up the naked Veronika, another one stopped at Todd, who was naked up to the waist. They were lying on the lawn in a park near their house.

"I am… I… wiz…" Veronika began explaining, raking around in search of her clothes. The two police officers gave each other puzzled looks.

"We love each other and wanted to make love, sir!" Todd said, interrupting the girl. He finally found his shirt, lying next to him, and covered Veronika with it.

She understood what he had said and, smiling and feeling embarrassed, nodded in confirmation of his words.

The guardians of law and order looked like they were hesitating. Once again, they carefully examined the young couple from head to toe and, casting a few quick glances around, concluded. "So, everything is all right? Okay then."

Having turned off their flashlights, the cops delicately left. Todd and Veronika were rolling on the ground, laughing. Todd tried to explain to Veronika that they got off easy because it was prohibited to make love in public places in the States, but she only laughed, not really listening to what he was talking about. Giving up on the explanations, Todd hugged Veronika and covered her with himself.

In the following days, they mostly just made love, either on the roof of the apartment complex, in the pool if there was nobody there, or in the nearest forest, right on the grass. Todd taught his girlfriend how to drive a sports car, told her about American rappers, had her listen to their music, and took her to clubs and restaurants. Veronika was happy and enjoyed all this romantic stuff until one day her boyfriend told her that he had signed up for the Air Force.

"What does this mean? Will they send you to war?" Veronika was horrified.

"No, silly. Here they recruit people into the military on a voluntary basis, and if there is no war—and now there isn't one—they teach you a specialty of your choice and pay for your school," Todd smiled meaningfully. "I don't have money for school; you probably know that education here is not free. And they pay for your house if you are married! So... if we get married, we will live in our own home together and happily ever after! What do you think? We'll get a dog and a cat, like you want! And we'll have kids," he patted her on the cheek. "Will you marry me, little one?"

'This is how Sasha used to call me...' thought Veronika. Little one was only a year younger and wasn't planning to get married at nineteen. But she wanted an adult life and adventures so much that without hesitation, she answered "yes" to her American prince. A week later, they rushed to Fort Covington in northern New York, where Tom's parents lived and where he had grown up. Before getting married and being sent to Columbus, Mississippi for military training, Todd wanted Veronika to meet his parents.

With a few short stops, the trip took almost a full day. Veronika kept gazing at the small and big cities from the car window, fantasizing about which ones she would like to live in.

Fort Covington turned out to be disappointing even before they got there. After sunny, friendly, clean Atlanta, Veronika didn't expect to see old ramshackle houses, half-destroyed gas stations, and endless fields, where thin, ill-nourished cows grazed. Fort Covington seemed like a dead, sad village to Veronika. However, she was so exhausted and hungry that she had neither the strength nor the desire to think about what she was seeing. Besides, Todd had already parked at the small house where his parents lived. Veronika crawled out of the car after her fiancé, who was now impatiently ringing the doorbell. An old woman opened the door.

"Mom!" Todd shouted cheerfully, throwing himself at her. "This is my bride! Her name is Veronika!"

His mother looked at him in shock. As it turned out, he didn't even think to let his parents know that he wouldn't be coming alone but with a girl, and not just some girl but his future wife. She invited them into the house with a confused gesture. Going out to meet the unexpected guests, Todd's father was no less shocked and, not understanding what was happening, looked at his son and then at his girlfriend, then back at his son. Not noticing their reaction, Todd poured out the news. Veronika was not just his girlfriend and not just a bride to be, but a bride from Russia! From the former Union of Soviet Socialist Republics! Veronika was modestly standing behind him all this time.

Fortunately, Todd's mother and father turned out to be

friendly and hospitable. Having recovered from the shock, they accepted Veronika as if she were their own daughter. Todd's father began improving her English. She liked to chat with her boyfriend's dad and enjoyed his company. But when he offered to teach her to shoot deer and partridges in a forest area that he had bought, Veronika flat out refused. She told him in English, which, thanks to their daily practice, had slightly improved, "If I need it for self-defense, I will shoot a man on the spot, but I won't kill a helpless animal!"

He shrugged and put the hunting rifle in the safe.

Todd's mother took on the trouble of preparing for the wedding. She drove Veronika to the shops and along the way, they stopped by the farms of their many relatives in the village. The owners proudly showed Todd's Russian bride their possessions: cows, horses, pigs and sheep. Veronika smiled politely. She didn't mind the detailed instructions of her fiancé's mother about how to cook venison or hot hearty breakfasts for her husband, how to greet him from work, and how to care for him. Veronika hadn't expected that she would be taught all this in America, where the ideas of women's liberation had been dominant for a long time, but she made allowances for Todd's mother's age and for life in general in this 'village away from civilization', as she called it.

Veronika was thinking more about the upcoming wedding, which she and Todd decided to have on a mountain in Lake Placid, near the highest mountain in the state of New York.

"Can we really do that? Hold a wedding on a mountain?" worried Veronika.

"Of course," Todd laughed. "Everything is possible in America! What kind of dress do you want?"

"The whitest and the most beautiful!" Veronika clapped her hands.

"You are my miracle!"

***

"Never, not even in my worst nightmare, could I have imagined that my son would marry a Russian!" Todd's mother Beth confessed to Veronika's father, when they were toasting, by no means the first glass of champagne, to the newlyweds.

The woman's thoughtful gaze was aimed at the bride and groom, who stood there, holding each other accepting congratulations. Veronika was glowing: everything had turned out just like she wanted and planned. In her gorgeous snow-white and puffy dress, to the applause of her parents and guests, she exchanged wedding vows and rings with the kindest, funniest, and very best man—her amazing Todd— in one of the most romantic places in the state.

"You know, I worked as a nurse in Vietnam," Beth continued, "and my husband was there, participating in that massacre. Robert still doesn't say anything about what happened over there. He can't even tell me. And now our children are going together to an American military base. How should we feel about this?" she looked inquiringly at Veronika's father, but he only nodded and smiled, embarrassed for not being able to maintain a complicated conversation in English.

***

Just as the army had promised, Veronika and Todd lived in a big house, for which they weren't paying a dime. Still, it was completely empty, except for a double mattress, lying on the living room floor, and a TV that was not connected to any cable channels and was intended for Nintendo—Todd played games in his spare time. One of the rooms, where the couple's bedroom was supposed to be, was littered with games, on which Todd wasted quite a bit of his modest military salary. He spent the rest of the money on his brand-new sports car and fancy audio system. He gave his young wife the very minimum for their household, which was enough to buy cheap food at the local grocery store.

Veronika, however, didn't complain. After an almost impoverished life in the Soviet Union and with its collapse in 1991 (Veronika was twelve then), in even poorer Russia, she truly thought that she and Todd were living in abundance. Yes, she wanted to buy some nice clothes, but there was no such thing as winter in Mississippi, and they didn't have to worry about warm clothing. And she had enough clothes for summer, spring and autumn—her mother brought her a whole wardrobe of dresses and shoes, which she had initially bought for herself when she moved to Atlanta. Luckily, they wore the same size.

The only thing that concerned Veronika was the promise of getting a cat and a dog that Todd didn't keep. He kept saying that they didn't have enough money to get pets. Just like Veronika's mother used to tell her all her childhood...

Veronika did not give up. She learned English well enough to go to college and attended the branch that was located at their military base. Veronika, for whom a B in Russia was a great achievement, began studying with great passion. She liked that American teachers praised her. At first, she felt constrained in front of a rather large audience because of her accent. But pretty much all the teachers told her what a great and smart student she was, and Veronika became more confident. She read her essays aloud during speech classes with such ardor and passion that her teacher advised her to think about a career in theatre.

"You have a gift for conveying your thoughts to others! With your manner of speaking, expressing yourself, with your facial expressions, with your charisma, you must perform on the stage!"

Realizing that she shouldn't wait for a cat or a dog from her husband, Veronika decided to act and, therefore, began looking for work. She carefully read the newspaper ads and methodically called all the restaurants, stores, and bars that had vacancies and didn't require special skills. Nobody ever called her back, and Veronika considered her Russian accent to be the reason.

***

This morning she opened her eyes to see a huge, black, hairy spider resting on her nose. Screaming did not scare it. Veronika jumped up and, still screaming, shook her head and stomped her feet till she finally shook it off—what a pest it turned out to be!

These huge creatures were everywhere here. Local

spiders were even worse than the 10-foot snakes that often crawled across the road when she walked to the store or college.

'Spring is my favorite time of the year, when green leaves blossom on the trees, streams flow, and everything wakes up after a prolonged sleep and comes to life.' Veronika thought about that a little and in the next instant, burst out laughing. 'Yeah, comes to life!'

Veronika shivered, but immediately got her thoughts together and quickly began writing in her notebook. She had to hand in her essay on time because after class, she had a meeting at the modeling agency. Finally, she had been invited for an interview! According to the ad in the newspaper, to which she responded, they were looking for models to shoot commercials.

At 3PM sharp, Veronika confidently pushed open the glass doors of the large modern building on Main Street, where the modeling agency office was located.

"Hello, my name is Veronika," she announced to a very beautiful black girl, who was sitting at the table. Judging by her looks, they were about the same age. "I have a meeting with Alberto at three."

"Very nice to meet you. I'm Jacqueline. You can call me Jackie. Alberto will be with you in a couple of minutes. He's in the studio now, but he's already wrapping up. Take a seat, please. Can I offer you water, coffee, soda?"

"Oh, yes, can I have a Coke? Thank you!" Veronika sat in the chair, to which she was pointed. Jackie got up from the table and went into the next room. She was very tall and at the same time, delicate and moved gracefully, like a cat. Veronika looked at the photographs of the models hanging on the walls and didn't even notice that the girl returned and put a glass of the bubbling soda in front of her.

A pot-bellied man of about fifty was already coming down the stairs from the second floor.

"Hello, you must be Veronika? And I'm Alberto!" he introduced himself, extending his hand to the guest. In his other hand, he was holding a camera with a giant lens.

"Yes, that's me. Pleasure to meet you!" Veronika was very excited. She jumped up and shook his soft, chubby palm with slightly sweaty fingers.

"My God!" exclaimed the photographer and stepped back. "You are beautiful! How old are you?"

"Nineteen. And you?" Veronika didn't expect this question to pop out. It was as if it slipped out.

However, Alberto only laughed.

"I'm fifty-six! But let's keep this between us, okay?" and he laughed even louder. "So… now that we've met." Alberto examined her from head to toe. "Let's try to make some pictures. What do you say?"

Veronika nodded, and Alberto took her upstairs, where there was an impressive-looking studio.

"Come stand here," Alberto ordered, waving his head at the large green screen that was hanging in the center of the room. "Now, we'll create something fantastic! Try to pretend that you are very bored, but at the same time, look gorgeous!"

Veronika didn't quite understand the task, but still tried to do what the photographer asked of her.

"Perfect!" he exclaimed and started clicking his camera. "Fantastic!"

Veronika perked up. She made a bored face and a

languid smile and took the pose that she had seen in one of the photographs hanging in the studio downstairs.

"Yes! That's it! Wonderful!" Alberto was happy. "And now turn a little to the left! Great! Bare your shoulder! Give me a cute smile!"

Click-click-click! Veronika liked the sound of the camera. It was easy and fun doing this. Following the instructions of the "maestro," she spontaneously turned back and lifted the corners of her lips.

"Oh! Wait, wait! Freeze like that! Don't do anything else! You are stunning, my dear! Wait, I'll give you a hat! This will add something!"

The heavy Alberto rushed down the stairs and after half a minute, came back running, a little out of breath and carrying a black top hat.

"Here, put it on; it'll be amazing! Give me half a smile. Good! And look directly at the camera. Imagine it's your lover! Like you want to have sex with it! Show me your most seductive look! Yes! Now, look at the camera and be serious, but also flirt with it!"

Veronika laughed. It was fun watching Alberto, who was thrilled to pieces. She also really wanted to see the result of their work. Showing him passion and love, she imagined Sasha...

Alberto got seriously carried away. He clicked his camera nonstop, ran from corner to corner, crouched, then fell to the floor, pointing the lens from below, then immediately jumped up, grabbed a chair, and balanced on it to catch the angle from above.

"Imagine that you are a predator, a panther, and there's a fluffy white rabbit before you! And now be Bambi, you've lost your mother, and a shotgun is pointed at you! You are scared, defenseless... Yes, good, good! Now show me that you're a cuddly kitty! Your owner is scratching your ear, purr-purr-purr-meow... Excellent! And now be a furious bull, sweeping away everything in its path, angered by the bullfighter! Yes! No! You…" Alberto took a breath. "You're a stallion, just released! You joyfully prance to the horizon, to the shining sun! You are free, free!"

Veronika's heart began pounding at these words. Oh, now she really understood very well what freedom meant and what happiness was.

"I'm free," she whispered, and tears flowed down her cheeks.

"Stop. Freeze like that!" In one leap the photographer jumped to Veronika, aimed the camera directly at her face and took several shots in a row. "Bravo! You're a natural born actress!" Alberto lowered the camera and, looking at Veronika with adoration, exclaimed, "These pictures with tears of happiness will be a real hit, I'm telling you! It's just amazing how you got into character!"

After the photoshoot, Jackie told Veronika that they would call her as soon as the photos were ready and asked if she needed a taxi.

"No, thanks," Veronika politely declined because she had no money for a taxi. "I would like to call my husband. He will come pick me up."

"Okay, you can call from here," Jackie pointed to the landline phone.

Veronika dialed the home number. Todd didn't answer.

'Damn, where is he?' She got nervous, listening to his voice on the answering machine. 'And what the hell am I supposed to do now?'

Jackie noticed her worries.

"If you want, I can give you a lift," she offered with ease. "I have a car."

"Really? Thank you!" Veronika didn't know how to thank this kind-hearted beautiful girl and just repeated, "Thank you very much!"

"No problem!" reassured her Jackie. "I was going home, anyway. Where do you live?"

"I live at the base. My husband is military."

"Got it. So, we'll go to the base! I've never been there! Exciting!"

On the way there, Jackie told her that in the modeling agency, she shot commercials for local stores and was also Alberto's assistant: she went with him to business meetings and taught beginning models to pose and walk the runway. She lived with five younger brothers, a sister, and her mother, who had three jobs, but the family still barely got by. Jackie had been working while going to school since she was fifteen, and last year, she got into the university to become a psychologist.

Jackie kept just one memory of her father. She was then two years old. She got thirsty and ran to the kitchen, where her father was sitting with a bottle of Jack Daniels, reclined in a chair. Hearing the daughter's request, he grunted, got up, staggering, went to the sink, poured water into the glass, from which he had previously drank whiskey, and threw some ice in it from the freezer. Over the evening, he got pretty loaded and didn't realize that his baby daughter couldn't drink from such glasses yet. A piece of ice stuck in her throat, she began choking, turned red, but couldn't utter a sound and could only look at her father with wide eyes.

"It'll melt." He waved his hand, leaned back in his chair, and sipped from the bottle.

"Father was right," Jackie said with a grin. "As you can see, I'm alive and well, but that very day, my mother kicked that drunk out of the house, and I never saw him again. I had a stepfather. I loved him dearly; only he died a few years ago."

While Jackie was telling her story, Veronika managed to take a closer look at her. She was incredibly good-looking. In addition to her amazing figure: slender and flexible, yet not without seductive curves, she had the finest, Veronika would even say angelic, features. She had big almond-shaped eyes, thick, long eyelashes, wonderful wavy black hair, full, well-defined lips, and delightful smile.

Her plain clothes only emphasized her natural beauty. Probably the only bright thing on Jackie was a rather massive watch that she wore on her right wrist. Veronika noticed it when she got into the car. Mickey Mouse looked out from the dial. It was almost the same as on her first watch. Veronika's heart skipped a beat: she had it on that evening, in Anatoly's apartment, and it stayed there. Either it came undone, or the strap broke when those bastards… Veronika shook her head, chasing away the memories. She didn't want to think about the past now and shifted her attention back to Jackie.

All the way to the base, the girls chatted nonstop. Veronika admired her new friend; she liked her liveliness, sincerity, and openness, and the fact that Jackie did not seem to care about Veronika's accent. Veronika told Jackie a little about herself: that she came from Russia, got married here, went to college at the military base, and that her teachers advised her to think about a theatrical career. And Alberto, by the way, also said that! Veronika described to Jackie that one moment during the photo shoot, when he asked her to pretend she was a stallion that had been freed, and how she burst into tears. She didn't explain the true cause of those tears.

"Listen," Jackie responded immediately, "talk to Alberto! You see, he knows lots of people. There must be someone he knows who can help you with acting classes. Alberto is awesome! Although he has a foul mouth during his photo shoots, truth is, he just likes to have fun and is passionate about his work. He's also a great husband and father! He adores his Louise and their four sons."

"How cool is that we're going to the base!" exclaimed Jackie when they turned onto the road that led to the gate. "I love men in uniform so much! I always dreamed of a boyfriend who would serve in the Air Force. I'm single now," she said cheerfully, "and before that I was with one guy who turned out to be a complete asshole! I caught him with my best friend, so I told her 'Girl, BYE!'" Jackie took a breath. "And we had been friends since we were little. I can't believe that snake... If only she had called and apologized—but no! She's not with that moron anymore, but she's not trying to make amends with me, either. Damn..." Jackie sighed and suddenly concluded. "Ah, to hell with her!"

Veronika thought of her only friend, to whom she hadn't spoken for a very long time.

'Alina, of course, was somewhat right,' she thought,

'but too selfish. Chasing after nonexistent millionaire princes. Ugh!' She frowned. Suddenly, she felt it all going, even the fact that Alina hadn't taken a single step toward reconciliation. 'To hell with her!' Veronika decided for herself following Jackie's example.

The black-skinned beauty was already happily waving to the military guard at the checkpoint, at which they had just arrived.

"Hello! I'm Jackie! Taking this precious cargo back home on your base!"

Veronika smiled at the guards, whom she knew well. They nodded ceremoniously and gestured that they could drive through.

"Wow, how easy it was to get into the holy of holies!" remarked Jackie with complete irony. "Where to now?"

"Straight, and then turn right at the light."

Jackie drove up to the house, and Veronika, who didn't want to part with her merry new friend, invited her to come inside.

"I'd love to, but not now," Jackie looked honestly disappointed about it. "It's too late. I have to go home. Need to help my mother put the little ones to sleep. She comes in for a short break after one job and then goes to another on a night shift. She's a nurse—well, I already told you. I'll call you soon, we'll hang out! Okay?"

"Ok! It's nice meeting you."

"Likewise, girl!" Jackie flashed her dazzling smile, and Veronika got out of the car.

"Wait a minute!" Jackie called to her and, bending over the passenger seat, peaked out of the open window. She held out her watch to Veronika. "Take it! I'm giving it to you. I saw how you looked at it all the way here."

Veronika felt embarrassed. "Don't be silly! It's just... I had a similar watch once with Mickey..."

"Even better. There you go! I really want you to have it," Jackie slipped Veronika the watch, winked, sent her an air kiss, and hit on the gas.

***

Todd was at home. Veronika found him in front of the TV screen with a game. He was intently following the score, nervously clutching the joystick in his hands, and paid no attention to her.

"Hey! Hello!" Veronika called out to her husband, taking off her shoes and gazing at Jackie's present. The watch really looked like hers, only this Mickey was in color, not black-and-white, and there was a tiny round window with a tiny compass arrow inside the dial.

Todd mumbled something inarticulate, frantically manipulating the handle.

"Earth to Todd! I went to a modeling agency!"

"Yeah, okay, good, honey..."

"I had a real photo shoot. I got accepted, and they told me that they will soon call me back with the results!" Veronika shared the news.

"Yep..."

"I met Jackie! She is such a great girl! She is the assistant to the owner-photographer and a model for the same agency," continued Veronika, already realizing that she was addressing the air.

"Cool!" Todd still couldn't take his eyes off the game.

Veronika glanced at the phone: the answering machine was blinking red, which meant that he didn't even check her message.

"I called you—were you at home?"

"Yep."

Veronika made one last attempt to reach him.

"I ate a snake!"

"Yes, yes, baby, fine," Todd muttered as if under hypnosis, staring at the screen. He was shooting another batch of green aliens, and he clearly didn't have time for his wife's stories.

Veronika was almost used to Todd's gaming sessions, so she expressed only slight annoyance, making a face at the back of his head, and ran off to the kitchen. There, on the floor, was a box with a couple of dried-up pizza slices. 'Such a caring husband!' Veronika sarcastically noted to herself. She picked up a piece and, barely chewing the cold dough with a crust of frozen cheese, thought, 'Okay, now we'll give you the show of the century!'

She took a quick shower, wrapped herself in a towel, let her hair down, and entered the room where her husband was still sitting.

"Would you like to experience unearthly pleasure, sir?" she asked in a low, sexy voice and dropped the towel.

"Sure, give me a sec, baby!" Todd mumbled. He didn't even look up at his young wife, carried away by his fight with the space enemies.

Veronika was hurt and thoroughly angry. With a sudden movement, she picked up the towel from the floor and left the room, saying to herself out loud.

"That's it! I'm going to bed!" and, remembering

Jackie's words, added in a quieter voice. "BYE, dear husband!"

Todd didn't even turn his head.

Curling up on the mattress, Veronika lay in bed for a long time, reciting her day in her head. She eventually dreamed of a wild red stallion. Excited that he had learned to run, he was joyously galloping through the sunlit meadow. At some point, though, he realized that he was lost and began rushing about in the tall grass, not knowing, which way to go. He saw a white rabbit sneak past him, chased by a panther. Then a huge snake crawled before him. He heard an invisible bull bellow somewhere very close. And finally, a huge, red veil fell upon them all from the sky. The shining sun disappeared, and darkness fell. The stallion was trapped…

Veronika woke up and opened her eyes. She was still lying alone on the mattress. The light from the screen was still flickering in Todd's game room.

'Is it possible to experience the joy of freedom if you have never been deprived of it? And is it possible to feel inner freedom if you have never felt trapped in your own brain?'

Without thinking this through, she fell asleep again.

***

The next day, Veronika got up with a vague feeling of anxiety. 'It's probably just me feeling lonely,' she thought while she was taking a shower.

Veronika didn't call her grandparents often because phone calls to Russia were expensive, but today she really wanted to hear their voices. Before she even had breakfast, she ran to the store to buy a phone card.

"Darling honey!" Once she heard their dear voices on the phone, she was overwhelmed with tenderness. "We miss you so much! How are you, sweetie? When will you come visit us?" they kept asking, interrupting each other.

"I'm all right, Granny! I also miss you both so very much." She didn't want to tell them that she didn't have the money for a ticket. That would make them upset.

"Honey," her grandmother hesitated, "we have very bad news. Sasha... he died."

Veronika's heart sank. Everything went dark before her eyes.

"What do you mean, died?"

"Yes, dear, it just happened... this morning. Sasha's grandfather told us. He died of pneumonia. But we think that he overdosed, or maybe it was his disease; after all, he had AIDS."

Veronika's hands and feet went cold. Her temples started throbbing. Sasha? Her Sasha? Her childhood friend, her love, even if he was with another... died?

Veronika fell onto the mattress and, sobbing, repeated into the phone,

"How could it be? How? Why?"

When Todd returned from work, Veronika was still lying on the mattress, with her face buried in the pillow and her hands wrapped around it. She had been crying uncontrollably for several hours, but the tears just wouldn't stop.

"Is something wrong? What happened?" Todd asked. He looked worried. She looked up at him with her red, swollen eyes and, without saying anything, burst into tears again.

"Hey!" Todd shook Veronika by the shoulder. She howled, choking on tears, and didn't react to his touch. Apprehensively Todd dialed 911 and yelled into the phone,

"My wife has been crying nonstop for hours! I don't understand what's wrong with her! I think she's having a meltdown. I don't know what to do!"

"Can you hear me?" the operator spoke calmly and clearly. "Stay with your wife; we're sending a team."

Two minutes later, the siren of the ambulance was heard approaching the house. Todd opened the door to the paramedics, pointed at his wife, who was still sobbing, lying face down on the mattress. Indifferent to everything, Veronika let them examine her, and when the paramedics told Todd that she had very high blood pressure and needed to go to the hospital, she just obediently sat on the stretcher. Nervously biting his lips, Todd handed his wife her handbag.

In the emergency room, Veronika was sedated. When she woke up, she saw a black woman in scrubs by her bed. The woman's face was calm and strict. She asked her what had happened.

"My friend is dead. My best friend is dead... And I wasn't there to help him..."

"I'm very sorry for your loss," the doctor said warmly. "How are you feeling now?"

"Bad... I feel really bad. It hurts so much."

The doctor carefully looked at Veronika.

"Do you have suicidal thoughts?"

"No, but I was feeling depressed long before that."

"Are you having trouble in your relationships?"

"Yes"

"Do you feel sad, guilty?"

"Yes. Yes! That's exactly how I feel!"

"Do you want to be admitted to the hospital?"

"What does that mean?"

"It means that you will be taken to a different hospital. There you will be able to talk to some specialists, who will help you deal with your grief and depression."

"Okay."

The stretcher appeared again, and they told her to lie down. Veronika tried to convince the nurses that she had calmed down and could walk by herself.

"You have to lie down. It's protocol," they explained to her.

And she did.

Veronika was taken to an ambulance, the stretcher rolled into the back with two nurses by her side, and when they arrived at the destination, they again told her not to get up. They carefully rolled the stretcher out. She heard the folding cart clang beneath her and felt a weak jolt when the wheels touched the ground. They took her down to the gate, behind which there was a big gray building. The gates opened automatically and, then they closed. At the front door, one of the aids punched in a code. Veronika was surprised at such security, but because of the sedative, she was a bit slow and, therefore, remained still.

The door of the room, where they finally brought her, immediately slammed shut behind them, and the approaching nurses, not the ones, who had escorted her, but other ones, asked if she could get up.

"Yes, of course!" Veronika answered, getting down from the stretcher.

"Will you let me take your bag?"

"No!" Veronika pressed her handbag against her chest. "Why do you need it?"

"We need to check if you're trying to smuggle in any prohibited goods. And your clothes, too. You need to change, and there are some clothes prepared for you. Please take off the watch, you can get it later."

'Am I in a mental hospital? No, that can't be...' She couldn't think straight. She gave them her bag and watch and went to the changing room. Slowly pulling on some sort of loose blue garment, she again started thinking about Sasha, seemed to come to her senses, and looked around, trying to understand where she was. 'I really am in a loony bin. Oh, my God!'

"What now?" Veronika asked, leaving the room. A young nurse was already waiting for her. He said that his name was Paul and that he would take her to her room and show her what else was there. He then gave Veronika back her things. She grabbed her handbag, pressed it with her elbow to her side, tightly fastened the watch strap on her wrist and followed Paul down the corridor.

"This is the recreation room," the nurse pointed to the open door. Veronika looked into the doorway and froze: an old, scary-looking woman was staring at her with black, empty eyes, muttering something under her breath. Shocked by the image, Veronika barely managed to look away and hurried after Paul. The old woman's rattling loud voice followed her.

"Demons, they brought demons! Keep your eyes open!

The devil has come to us. Lord, forgive me."

They walked past the large, glazed hall for group therapy and past the office of the head physician.

"And here is your room, Veronika." Paul pushed the door. "You will share it with a roommate."

Veronika stared at the two beds and the table between them, and it finally dawned on her: she really was in an asylum!

"No, no!" she cried out, turning to the nurse. "You misunderstood me! I'm not crazy! I don't have to be here!"

"Yes, yes, of course, I understand," the aid responded in an apologetic tone. "Make yourself comfortable." Without letting her say anything, he left.

'Jesus, where am I?' Veronika instantly remembered the scenes from *One Flew over the Cuckoo's Nest*. 'This is a nightmare. All the psychos, when they are put in a nuthouse, insist that they are not crazy! God, how do I get out of here?'

Veronika thought for a while and then rushed to the office of the head physician. It was empty, but the nurse who had previously escorted her, was already walking toward her.

"May I help you?"

"Yes! Listen to me!" Veronika began explaining disconnectedly. "Maybe I don't quite understand, and my English isn't perfect, but I got here by mistake!"

"What do you mean?" Paul asked in a calm voice.

Veronika broke down.

"Da blyad!" she yelled in Russian. "Tvoyu mat! Pozvonite moemu muzhu! Ya ne khochu zdes ostavatsa! Ya ne sumasshedshaya!"

"I don't understand you." The nurse tensed up.

"A ya, blyad, vas ne ponimayu! Call my husband!"

"Okay, okay, I'll call the doctor. Please, calm down."

"I don't need a doctor! Call my husband, he will explain everything to you!"

"I have to call the doctor," Paul repeated, not taking his eyes off her. "And you will explain everything to him yourself. Now, please go back to your room."

Veronika was genuinely scared. They considered her insane here, and now they would lock her up in this madhouse and force-feed her pills, from which she would turn into a vegetable with no emotions, thoughts, or feelings.

"No, no!" she cried in despair. "I won't go to any room! Give me back all my things and let me go home! Now!"

The other nursing technicians ran up to Veronika.

"Are you okay?"

"No, I'm not okay! I mean, yes, I'm fine! I mean, I'm not crazy! I got here by mistake! Call my husband! Let me go home!"

She knew that she needed to stop, just stop this hysterical fit right now. Otherwise, they would give her something to calm her down. She had seen this in the movies more than once, but shock and fear caused her to completely lose control, and she just kept screaming.

"Call my husband right now! He will explain everything to you! You can see, I don't speak English good, and this is a mistake. I should not be here!"

However, the aides who had surrounded her didn't try to sedate her. They only asked her monotonously and politely to calm down. Instead of her room, where Veronika refused to go, they offered to let her sit in the recreation room while they were dealing with the situation. She stopped yelling and followed the nurse. Fortunately, the mad old woman with black eyes wasn't in the room anymore. Veronika sat on the edge of an empty chair and looked around. Two young men were playing chess next to her.

"Hey, buddy!" said one of them. He had a long beard and a kind face although his expression was somewhat strange. "Don't you see my wife? Don't sit on her lap!" He giggled.

"What? Your wife? Where?" Veronika stared blankly at the man.

"What do you mean 'where'? In the chair you're sitting in! Can't you see her?"

Veronika jumped up and looked at the chair, as if there really were someone there other than she.

"But it's empty!" she said, confused.

The bearded man laughed.

'My God, he's really crazy!' thought Veronika. She wrapped her hands around herself and looked at the second man, who looked Latino. He winked cheerfully and introduced himself.

"I am Jimmy. Don't mind my friend."

'Whew, at least this one isn't nuts!' Veronika moved to a different chair and smiled politely. "Hi, I'm Veronika."

"Nice to meet you!"

"My name is Jonathan, and my wife is Su-yako!" the bearded one interrupted them and looked fondly at the empty chair. "Where are you from?"

"Russia."

"Oh," he said, getting noticeably excited. "Russia! I

love commies! I'm also a communist at heart!"

"Yes, yes, it's very interesting," Veronika said, stretching her lips into a forced smile, and prayed to herself. 'God, God, help me!'

Jonathan dropped the chess board, turned to Veronika, and spoke rapidly.

"I was born in Cuba! In 2040, I brought my wife, my children, a parrot, a dog and a horse here. We weren't fleeing from the communists! We just decided to move here, because my uncle left me an inheritance, this kingdom! Of course, the capitalist system is, you know, not my thing, but when a palace, a stable, and servants passed to you as inheritance, it's hard to decline!"

Veronika was utterly shocked, looking at Jonathan, then at Jimmy. The latter gave her a big wink, as if to cheer her up.

"Uh... this is wonderful," Veronika muttered, not knowing how else to respond.

"My wife is Japanese," the bearded man ranted, not paying attention to Veronika. "She, as you can see, is very beautiful and doesn't talk much. She won't make a scene if someone doesn't notice her and sits in her place or even on top of her, as you did. Now let me tell you!" he enthusiastically slapped himself on the knees. "Last night we were making love, and one of our servants entered without knocking. He needed, apparently, to check if everything was all right, because Su-yako was screaming— screaming with passion! Of course, it's simply outrageous that he came in, but I can understand him: my wife is always so quiet, and then she suddenly screams like that!" Jonathan giggled and looked at Veronika mysteriously. "Well, of course, I told the servant that everything was fine, and he left." But did he spoil the mood or what, ha-ha-ha! I think now I will have to fire him. But then again, I'm not entirely sure."

Veronika's head was spinning from this endless torrent of words, but the bearded man continued pouring out information.

"Yes, I'm not sure! Because, on the one hand, he was fulfilling his duties—he was guarding the territories entrusted to him, and on the other, he interrupted us, breaking into our bedroom! What do you think?" He suddenly turned to Veronika.

"Um…" Veronika still had no idea what to say and looked hopefully at Jimmy. He quickly came to the rescue.

"I told ya, don't pay any attention to my friend! He's just very jealous. Jealous of his wife for no reason, jealous of the servant, of me. And of you, too! Well, you did sit on her lap, after all, but she is really very beautiful. How can he not be jealous?"

Veronika's eyes nearly popped out of her head.

'Well, here we go, this one's crazy, too. But they don't even look like psychos… God, what's going on! I'm gonna go crazy, too! Someone get me out of here!'

Nurse Paul entered the room and asked whether everything was fine.

"Did you call my husband?"

"Mmm, your husband is not answering our calls. Maybe you gave us the wrong number?"

"No, I gave you the right number! That asshole is just playing video games. That's why he won't answer!"

"Well, that means he will call us back soon. We left a